Lionel S. Beale

Protoplasm

life, force, and matter

Lionel S. Beale

Protoplasm
life, force, and matter

ISBN/EAN: 9783337776190

Printed in Europe, USA, Canada, Australia, Japan

Cover: Foto ©Andreas Hilbeck / pixelio.de

More available books at **www.hansebooks.com**

PROTOPLASM;

Life, Force, and Matter.

ὀλιγοδρανέες, πλάσματα πηλοῦ, σκιοειδέα φῦλ’ἀμενηνά.

ARISTOPH. *Aves*, 686.

PROTOPLASM;

OR,

LIFE, FORCE, AND MATTER.

BY

LIONEL S. BEALE, M.B., F.R.S.,

Fellow of the Royal College of Phyficians : Phyfician to King's College Hofpital.

WITH

NUMEROUS COLOURED DRAWINGS, EXECUTED ON WOOD, AND COPIED
FROM THE OBJECTS THEMSELVES.

LONDON:

J. CHURCHILL & SONS, NEW BURLINGTON STREET.

1870.

_{*} The degree of amplifying power used is stated at the foot of each figure in *diameters*, or *linear measure*. × 500, means that the representation is 500 times longer or wider, measured in one direction only, than the object itself. If the object was 1 inch in length, the drawing would extend over 500 inches, or would be 41 feet 8 inches long.

The diameter of any object can be ascertained by comparison with the scales at the foot of each plate.

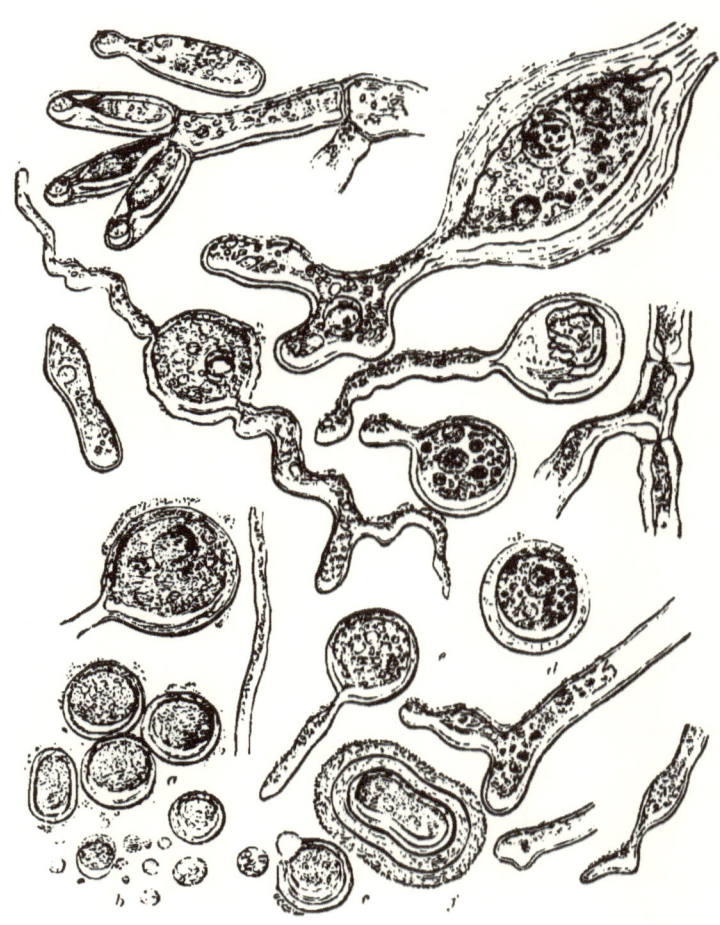

In this drawing the germinal or living matter of mildew during growth is represented. The figures have been copied from specimens well stained by immersion in carmine fluid. *a*, spores protected by a thick layer of formed material. *b*, smallest particles of germinal or living matter within; any one of these minute particles might grow. *c*, a spore bursting; germinal matter escaping. *d*, a spore enlarged by growth. *e*, a spore sprouting. *f*, an old spore, the formed material of which has been much thickened by the formation of new layers within. The remaining figures show the growth of the long filaments (mycelium) and the fructification of the fungus. It will be noticed that in all these changes the germinal matter only takes part. The formed material is perfectly passive, and does not grow. Magnified 1700 diameters.

PHYSICAL LIFE AND ITS BASIS.

HE opinion that life is a form or mode of energy or motion has for many years past been gaining an increased number of advocates, and now appears to be very generally entertained and taught by scientific men. The idea that life is a power, force, or property of a special and peculiar kind, temporarily influencing matter and its ordinary forces, but entirely different from, and in no way correlated with these, has been ridiculed, and is often spoken of as if it were too absurd to require refutation. And yet it is doubtful if any one who has carefully studied the matter is fully satisfied as to the accuracy of the facts, and the cogency of the arguments advanced in favour of the physical doctrine of life. Nay, do not very positive affirmations, if unsupported by well-demonstrated facts, suggest to the reader a suspicion whether after all, the writer himself is, thoroughly con· vinced of the truth of the doctrine to which he has committed himself, and which he has determined to advo· cate with all the force of his authority, and to the very utmost of his power?

It may be that facts recently discovered strongly support

B

this now popular notion: it may be that the tendency of modern research is, as has been said, indubitably and strongly in this direction,—but some of us cannot feel satisfied that this is really so. Surely it is not too much to ask that the exact way should be pointed out in which new facts afford support to the doctrine, and that we should be furnished with something more definite to guide our reason than what is called the "*tendency*" of investigation, of thought, or opinion; for this "tendency," when carefully analyzed, will sometimes be found to amount only to this, that certain influential persons have determined that a particular opinion shall be widely taught, or a particular theory agreed upon shall be expounded and diffused as widely and as quickly as possible.

Disclaiming authority of every kind, the adherents of the new school of opinion profess to influence others, and to be influenced themselves, by reason alone. But by urging " the tendency of investigation" and " the spirit of modern thought" in favour of doctrines they cannot support by evidence, they appeal to the shadow of an authority which they affect to despise. Every student has undoubted right to require that scientific doctrines, which he is asked and expected to accept as true, should be supported by facts rather than by the authority of tendencies and prophecies. In favour of regarding living beings as mere machines built by force alone, maintained and preserved by force, and even created by force, it is true, very positive statements have been made; but these have been, for the most part, supported by arguments more ingenious than conclusive. I for one am ready to accept these views, no matter what change in opinions, beliefs, or hopes that acceptance may involve, provided only they are shown to rest upon facts of observation and experiment. But should mere authority alone induce any conscientious, thoughtful man, who has devoted himself to the study of nature, to believe and confess that a living, moving, growing thing is but a force-created, force-impelled machine? When we watch the lowest forms of living matter under high magnifying powers, do we learn anything to justify us in accepting such a view? When we ask our confident teachers of the new philosophy to assist us, we get dogmatic assertions, but nothing by way of explanation. Grand words are freely used, but the terms employed are not defined. It is, however, true enough, that men eminent among philosophers, as well as some of the most distinguished living physicists, chemists, and naturalists, have accepted this physical theory of life. They have taught that life is but a mode of ordinary force, and that the living thing differs from the non-living thing, not in quality, or essence, or kind, but merely in degree ; and yet they cannot satisfactorily explain the difference between a living thing and the same thing dead. They would perhaps tell us that living and dead are only relative terms; that there is no *absolute* difference between the dead and living states ; and that the thing which we call *dead*, is, after all, only a few degrees less actively living than the thing we say is *alive*. But is this sort of reasoning convincing, seeing that although matter in the living state may suddenly pass into the dead state, this same matter can never pass back again into the living condition ? Those who advocate this doctrine do not believe in the actual annihilation of force, when a living thing suddenly passes from the living into the dead state; but they do not demonstrate the new form or mode which the departing life-energy assumes, or explain to us what in their opinion becomes of it. If the dead thing only differs from the living thing by a few degrees of heat or units of force, why can we not, by supplying more heat or force, prevent dissolution, or cause the actions to go on again after they have once stopped?

In fact this view has been supported by assertions instead of by facts, and of the arguments hitherto advanced in its favour by its most powerful advocates, all are inconclusive, and some quite unjustifiable. He who chooses may accept upon faith as an article of belief the dogma that all the actions of living beings are due to ordinary forces only; but it is absurd to put forward such a conclusion as if it had been proved, or as if it were in the existing state of knowledge capable of proof. So long as the advocates of the physical doctrine of life contented themselves with ridiculing "vitality" as a fiction and a myth, because it could not be made evident to the senses, measured or weighed, or proved scientifically to exist, their position was not easily assailed; but now when they assert dogmatically that vital force is only a form or mode of ordinary motion, they are bound to show that the assertion rests upon evidence, or it will be regarded by thoughtful men as one of a large number of fanciful hypotheses, advocated only by those who desire to swell the ranks of the teachers and expounders of dogmatic science, which, although pretentious and authoritative, must ever be intolerant and unprogressive.

PROFESSOR OWEN'S NEW VIEWS.

PROFESSOR OWEN has lately avowed his belief in the doctrine that the so-called vital forces are really ordinary physical forces. Unlike many advocates, however, he admits that "on one or two points" proof is wanting. But Owen goes much farther than the most advanced microscopical observers and scientific investigators. He maintains that the formation of living beings out of *inanimate matter*, by the conversion of physical and chemical into vital modes of force, is going on *daily and hourly!* The evidence he has adduced in favour of this strange view, it need scarcely be said, is scanty, uncertain, and unconvincing; while a mass of facts and arguments which have been adduced in favour of the opposite conclusion, *that every particle of living matter comes from a pre-existing particle*, has been unconsciously neglected or purposely ignored.

It is very significant that so great a master is unable to suggest a better instance of the analogy which he affirms exists between physical and vital actions than is afforded by magnetism. He says that there is nothing peculiar to living things in their power of *selecting* certain constituents, because a magnet *selects* also. Let the reader consider how different is the process called *selection* in these two cases. A magnet, says Owen, *attracts* towards it only certain kinds (a certain kind?) of matter. Is there, then, no difference between *selection* and *attraction?* Nor, he further observes, is death characteristic of things living only; for if the steel be unmagnetized, is it not "dead?" Devitalize the sarcode (living amœba), unmagnetize the steel, and both cease to manifest their respective vital or magnetic phenomena. In that respect both are "defunct." "Only," remarks the same authority, "the steel resists *much longer* the surrounding decomposing agencies;" and I would add, but <u>this</u> Owen would regard as a matter of the utmost indifference, you can unmagnetize and remagnetize the magnet as often as you like, but you can only kill the amœba once, and you can never revitalize it.

In answer to my objections to some of his statements, Professor Owen observes that " there are organisms (Vibrio Rotifer, Macrobiotus, &c.) which we can devitalize and revitalize—devive and revive—many times."* That such organisms can be *revived*, all will admit, but probably Professor Owen will be alone in not recognizing any distinction between the words *revitalizing* and *reviving.* The animalcule that can be *revived* has never been dead, but that which is not dead cannot be *revitalized.* The distinction between life and death must not be ignored. The half-drowned man that can be revived has never been dead.

How can there be any analogy whatever between the half desiccated quiescent animalcule and a completely desiccated dead animalcule, or a man dead from drowning? The one *lives*, and the others are *dead.* The difference between the living state and the dead state is absolute, for that which has once lost its life can never regain it.

* "The Monthly Microscopical Journal," No. V, May 1, 1869, p. 294.

If Owen regards the (apparently) dried animalcule as being, " as completely lifeless as is the drowned man whose breath and heat have gone, and whose blood has ceased to circulate," he will not find many to agree with him; for will not a drop of water resuscitate or revive the one, but who shall revitalize the other?

MR. GROVE ON EXPERIMENTAL ORGANISM.

MR. GROVE has recently* affirmed that "in a voltaic battery and its effects" we have "the nearest approach man has made to experimental organism:" but surely it should be shown in what particulars a voltaic battery resembles an organism. All organisms come from pre-existing organisms, and all their tissues and organs are formed from or by a little clear, transparent, structureless, moving matter which came from matter like itself, but may increase by appropriating to itself matter having none of its properties or powers. Now, voltaic batteries do not grow or multiply, nor do they evolve themselves out of structureless material, nor, if you give them ever so much pabulum in the shape of the constituents of which they are made, do they appropriate this. Where too is the chemist who gives what is selected? What then does Mr. Grove mean by asserting that a voltaic battery is the nearest approach man has made to experimental organism? Has man yet made the slightest approach to experimental organism? If any apparatus we could contrive developed all possible modes of force—motion, heat, light, electricity, magnetism, chemical action, and any number of others yet to be discovered—that apparatus would still present no approach whatever to any organism known. Of course such a thing might he *called* an organism, just as a watch, or water, or a gas, or an elementary substance may be called a creature, or a worm a machine; but everything that lives—every so-called living

* British Medical Journal, May 29, 1869, p. 486.

machine—grows of itself, builds itself up, and multiplies, while every non-living machine *is made, does not grow, and does not produce machines like itself.* Mr. Grove further says that in the human body we have chemical action, electricity, magnetism, heat, light, motion, and possibly other forces " contributing in the most complex manner to sustain that result of combined action which we call life." Here it seems to be affirmed that forces sustain the result of their own combined action, but surely this is only asserting that these forces sustain themselves. Heat, light, electricity, etc., sustain the result of the combined action of heat, light, electricity. It is moreover said that what we call *life* is the result of the combined action of motion, heat, light, electricity, etc., which are but different forms or modes of one force. But as everybody knows we may have any and all modes of force without life. Life therefore involves something besides force, or is something different from it.

PROFESSOR HUXLEY'S PHYSICAL BASIS OF LIFE.

IN order to convince people that the actions of living beings are not due to any mysterious vitality or vital force or power, but are in fact physical and chemical in their nature, Prof. Huxley gives to matter which is alive, to matter which is dead, and to matter which is completely changed by roasting or boiling, the very same name. The matter of sheep and mutton and man and lobster and egg is the same, and according to Huxley, one may be *transubstantiated* into the other. But how? By " subtle influences," and " under sundry circumstances," answers this authority. And all these things *alive,* or *dead,* or *roasted,* he tells us are made of protoplasm, and this protoplasm is the *physical basis* of life, or the basis of *physical life.** But can the discoverer of *" subtle influences"* afford to sneer at the fiction of vitality? By calling things which differ from one another in many qualities by the same name, Huxley annihilates distinctions, enforces identity, and sweeps away the difficulties which have impeded the progress of previous philosophers in their search after unity. Plants and worms and men are all protoplasm, and protoplasm is albuminous matter, and albuminous matter consists of four elements, and these four elements possess certain properties, by which properties all differences between plants and worms and men are to be accounted for. Although Huxley would probably admit that a worm was not a man, he would tell us that by " subtle

* The iron basis of the candle, and the basis of the iron candle are expressions evidently interchangeable.

influences" the one thing is easily converted into the other, and not by such nonsensical fictions as "vitality," which can neither be weighed, measured, nor conceived.

Some among those who work at and think over these matters doubt if many of Prof. Huxley's assertions are at all justified by his facts—unless indeed he has new facts of high importance which have not yet been brought forward—and many are unable to accept arguments which by him seem to have been considered quite conclusive. I shall therefore venture to draw attention to some of the views he has recently expressed in his paper, " On the physical basis of life," published in the *Fortnightly Review*, February 1st, 1869.

PROTOPLASM.

The term "Protoplasm" is now applied to several different kinds of matter,—to substances differing from one another in the most essential particulars. It seems, therefore, very desirable that its meaning should be accurately defined by those who employ it, or that it should be superseded by other words. If certain authorities were asked to define exactly the characters of the matter which they called protoplasm, we should have from those authors definitions applying to things essentially different from one another. Hard and soft, solid and liquid, coloured and colourless, opaque and transparent, granular and destitute of granules, structureless and having structure, moving and incapable of movement, active and passive, contractile and non-contractile, growing and incapable of growth, changing and incapable of change, animate and inanimate, alive and dead,—are some of the opposite qualities possessed by different kinds of matter which have nevertheless been called protoplasm.

A definition of protoplasm, most probably written by the late Professor Henfrey in " Griffith and Henfrey's Micrographic Dictionary," is as follows :—" *Protoplasm.*— The name applied by Mohl to the colourless or yellowish, smooth or granular viscid substance, of nitrogenous constitution, which constitutes the formative substance in the contents of vegetable cells, in the condition of gelatinous strata, reticulated threads and nuclear aggregations, &c. It is the same substance as that formerly termed by the Germans ' schleim,' which was usually translated in English works by ' mucus' or ' mucilage.' " The surface of this mass constituted the "formative protoplasmic layer" which was supposed to take part in the formation of the cellulose wall of the vegetable cell. This was regarded by Von Mohl as a structure of special importance distinct from the cell contents, and it was named by him, in 1844, the " primordial utricle."

In cases where protoplasm appears as a simple transparent homogeneous substance, several layers have been described, and it has been supposed that these different layers are concerned in different operations. This view has been extended to many forms of protoplasm, and the movements which occur have been attributed to the presence of two or more layers differing in density.

Clear, homogeneous protoplasm, it has been said, undergoes vacuolation, and becomes honeycombed, the spaces being filled with watery matter. In some instances, this change proceeds until mere protoplasmic threads are seen stretched across the cavity. The transparent fluid material occupying the spaces and the intervals between the threads is supposed to be the less important matter, and yet it is the living, growing, and moving substance; while the threads and walls of the spaces are composed of matter which has ceased to manifest these properties—matter which no longer lives, and which has been *formed from the living matter*. But we may fairly ask if this lifeless, passive, formed matter, which cannot move or grow or multiply of itself, which is but a product of the death of protoplasm, is nevertheless to be called by the same name as the living, moving substance which it once was? If this be so, there ought to be no recognizable difference between matter which is actually alive and the substances which result from its death.

So far, then, we have seen that the term protoplasm has been applied to the matter within the primordial utricle of the vegetable cell, to that clear substance which undergoes vacuolation and fibrillation, and to the matter forming the walls of the vacuoles and the threads or fibrillæ. Still more recently, Von Mohl's primordial utricle has been called protoplasm by Professor Huxley, who some years before restricted the term to the matter within the primordial utricle, which matter at that time he regarded as an "accidental anatomical modification" of the endoplast, and of little importance.* The nucleus, and with it the protoplasm, Mr. Huxley thought, exerted no peculiar office, and possessed no meta-

* "The Cell Theory," 'Med. Chir. Rev.,' October, 1853.

bolic power. Now, however, he considers " protoplasm " of the first importance; and under this term includes, I imagine, not only the primordial utricle and the " accidental anatomical modifications " it encloses, but the fully-formed cellulose wall of the vegetable cell. His *" endoplast"* and *"periplastic substance"* of 1853 together constitute his " protoplasm " of 1869. The old views are modified, and although the results of researches made during the last few years are scarcely alluded to, the writer evidently feels that certain changes must be made. So the vacuoles of the periplastic substance become silently tenanted by simple or nucleated protoplasms endowed with " subtle influences " which our author may yet admit to have existed before his periplastic substance was formed. Next he will discover the endoplast is of the highest importance instead of no importance at all, and then there is but an easy step to the doctrine that the *periplastic substance is formed by and from the protoplasm which has properties and " subtle influences" of a remarkable kind, but is not endowed with the absurd fiction of vitality.*

Max. Schultze included under the head of protoplasm the active moving matter forming the sarcode of the Rhizopods as well as the substance circulating in the cells of vallisneria, the hairs of the nettle, and other vegetable cells; and now it is generally admitted that the active, moving matter constituting the white blood-corpuscle, the mucus and pus corpuscle, and other contractile bodies widely distributed, is essentially of the same nature. The movements characteristic of this matter have been attributed to an inherent property of contractility; and this property has been held by some to be characteristic of, and peculiar to, protoplasm. Kühne considers all contractile material to be protoplasm, and includes the different forms of muscular tissue in the same category as the matter of the amœba, white blood-corpuscle, &c. But if we apply the term protoplasm to the contracting muscular tissue which exhibits *structure*, as well as to the living moving matter of the amœba, &c., in which no structure at all can be made out, it is obvious that these must be regarded as *essentially different kinds of protoplasm*, because they differ in properties which are essential and of the first importance. The contractile movement of the amœba, white blood-corpuscle, &c., is a phenomenon very different from the contraction of muscular tissue. In the first, movements occur in every direction, while the last is characterized by a repetition of movement in two definite directions only. And when we come to study the matter which is the seat of these two kinds of movements respectively, we find very important differences. The matter of the amœba, white blood-corpuscle, &c., grows. *It takes up matter unlike itself, and communicates to it its own properties.* Now, muscular tissue does not do this. In short, the first kind of matter acts and moves *of itself;* but the last can only *be acted upon and made to move.* The first may be compared to a spring, as yet undiscovered, which not only winds itself up and uncoils, but every part of which moves in any direction, and can make new springs out of matter which has none of the properties of a spring; the last to a spring which can only uncoil itself after it has been wound up.

Further, the term protoplasm has not been applied only

to the matter of which the amœba, the sarcode of the foraminifera, &c., is composed, and that which constitutes the white blood-corpuscle and such bodies, but the matter which is gradually assuming the form of tissue has been considered to be of the same nature. The radiating fibres of the caudate nerve-cells of the spinal cord have been termed protoplasm fibres, and the outer part of the nerve-cell with which they are continuous is composed of the same substance. The axis cylinder of the dark-bordered nerve-fibres and the fine ultimate nerve-fibres in peripheral parts have been looked upon as a form of protoplasm; but it is hardly necessary to remark that, whatever may be the nature of the material of which nerve-fibres and the outer part of nerve-cells are composed, it possesses properties very different from those manifested by the amœba, white blood-corpuscle, etc., and is destitute of the powers which characterize the matter constituting these bodies. Here again we find the term protoplasm applied to different kinds of matter or to matter in very different states.

But unfortunately we have by no means exhausted the confusion which has resulted with regard to protoplasm, for the name has been applied also to the outer, hard, dead part of epithelial cells and by implication to all corresponding structures.

Protoplasm of Huxley, 1869.

Up to this time all observers have agreed in opinion that the cell or elementary part of the fully-formed organism

consists of different kinds of matter, and it has been supposed that distinct offices were performed by some of these.
They have been variously named. Cell-wall, cell-contents,
nucleus, nucleolus, periplast, endoplast, primordial utricle,
protoplasm, living matter and formed matter, are not all the
terms that have been proposed. I think Professor Huxley
is the first observer who has spoken of the cell in its
entirety as a mass of protoplasm, and the only one who has
ever asserted that any tissue in nature is composed throughout of matter which can properly be regarded as one in
kind. This view appears to me incompatible with many
facts, some of which have been alluded to by Mr. Huxley
himself.* I doubt if in the whole range of modern science
it would be possible to find an assertion which seems more
at variance with facts familiar to physiologists than the
statement that "beast and fowl, reptile and fish, mollusk,
worm, and polype," are composed of "masses of protoplasm with a nucleus," unless it be that still more extravagant assertion that what is ordinarily termed a cell or
elementary part is a *mass of protoplasm;*—for can anything
be more unlike the semi-fluid, active, moving matter of
amœba protoplasm, than the hard, dry, passive, external
part of a cuticular cell or of an elementary part of bone?

I cannot forbear quoting in this place the following passage, which seems to me to require explanation. After
stating that the substance of a colourless blood-corpuscle

---

* "The original endoplast of the embryo cell," Huxley says, in
1853, "has grown and divided into all the endoplasts of the adult," and
"the original periplast has grown at a corresponding rate, and has
formed one *continuous and connected envelope* from the very first."

C

is an active mass of protoplasm, Mr. Huxley remarks that " *under sundry circumstances* the corpuscle dies and becomes distended into a round mass, in the midst of which is seen a smaller spherical body, which existed, but was more or less hidden in the living corpuscle, and is called its *nucleus*. Corpuscles of *essentially similar structure* are to be found in the *skin*, in the *lining of the mouth*, and scattered through the *whole framework of the body.*"　Now, what can be meant by a white blood-corpuscle dying and becoming distended into a round mass under sundry circumstances? Mr. Huxley goes on to say that at an early period of development the organism is " nothing but an aggregation of such corpuscles," that is, of corpuscles (elementary parts or cells) like those " found in the skin, in the lining of the mouth, and scattered through the whole framework of the body."　This assertion is incorrect, inasmuch as the corpuscles in the embryo consist almost entirely of (living) matter like the white blood-corpuscle, while those of which the skin (cuticle) and most of the tissues of the adult are composed consist principally of formed matter with a very little of the other (living) matter, while the oldest particles of cuticle are entirely composed of hard formed matter.　Here, as in other cases referred to by Huxley, no distinction is drawn between that which is *living, growing*, and *forming;* and that which has *been formed* and is *destitute of all powers of life and growth.*　No distinction between living matter and lifeless matter !　Both are confused together under the term " protoplasm," for which might be substituted " organic matter " or " albuminous matter."　Huxley terms the particles of epithelium of the cuticle and of mucous membranes, masses of protoplasm. He says beasts and fowls, reptiles and fishes, are all composed of structural units of the same character. Now, this mass of protoplasm, this unit, consists partly of *lifeless* and partly of *living* matter. The outer part, which may be dry and hard, and is lifeless, may be undergoing disintegration, and is perhaps being taken up by other living organisms, but is nevertheless, according to this view, just as much protoplasm as the living, growing, moving matter itself. It does not signify how many different things may be comprised in the cell or elementary part, in what essentially different states these things may be, how different parts may differ in properties—they constitute protoplasm. A muscle is protoplasm; nerve is protoplasm; bone, hair, and shell are protoplasm; a limb is protoplasm; the whole body is protoplasm, and of course bone, hair, shell, etc., are as much "the physical basis of life" as albuminous matter and roast mutton. But surely it would be less incorrect to speak of such "protoplasms" as the physical basis of *death* or the physical basis of *roast*, than to call dead and roasted matter the physical basis of *life*. No anatomical investigation is necessary to enable us to detect this substance. Every beast, fowl, reptile, worm, or polyp that we see is protoplasm. Everything that lives or has lived is protoplasm.

Bathybius.

I will now draw attention to a new form of protoplasm which has been much discussed of late, and concerning the nature of which much difference of opinion is entertained. From the protoplasm of the amœba and certain forms of foraminifera, we pass to larger and more extended masses of this substance, included under the head of "urschleim," and constituting the organisms of the simplest animated beings, which have been included by Hæckel in the genus *Moner.* I refer to this part of my subject with diffidence, for I have not given much attention to it. It would, however, be wrong to omit all mention of what is at the same time very interesting and of great importance. I shall therefore quote the observations of others so far as they appear to me to bear upon the consideration of the nature of protoplasm.

In the "Microscopical Journal" for October, 1868, is a memoir by Professor Huxley "On some Organisms living at great Depths in the North Atlantic Ocean," in which he states that the stickiness of the deep-sea mud is due to "innumerable lumps of a transparent gelatinous substance," each lump consisting of *granules, coccoliths,* and *foreign bodies,* imbedded in a "transparent, colourless, and structureless matrix." The granules form heaps which are sometimes the $\frac{1}{1000}$th of an inch or more in diameter. The "granule" is a rounded or oval disc, which is stained yellow by iodine, and is dissolved by acetic acid. "The granule heaps *and* the transparent gelatinous matter in which they are embedded represent masses of protoplasm." One of the masses of this deep-sea "urschleim" may be regarded as a new form of the simplest animated beings (*Moner*), and Huxley proposes to call it *Bathybius.* The "*Discolithi* and the *Cyatholithi,*" some of which resemble the "granules," are said to bear the same relation to the protoplasm of *Bathybius* as the spicula of sponges do to the soft parts of those animals ; but it must be borne in mind that the spicula of sponges are imbedded in a matrix, which is formed by and contains, besides the spicula, small masses of living or germinal matter. As in other cases, this matrix, with the living matter included, constitutes the "protoplasm" of Mr. Huxley.*

Dr. Wallich's Observations.

Dr. Wallich, has, however, arrived at a very different conclusion. In a paper "On the Vital Functions of the Deep-sea Protozoa," published in No. I. of the "Monthly Microscopical Journal," January, 1869, this observer, who has long been engaged in this and kindred studies, states that the coccoliths and coccospheres stand in no direct relation to the protoplasm substance referred to by Huxley under the name of *Bathybius*. The former are derived from their parent coccospheres, which are independent structures altogether. "*Bathybius,*" instead of being a *widely-extending living protoplasm* which grows at the expense of inorganic elements, is rather to be regarded as a complex mass of slime with many foreign bodies and the

---

* The idea of the existence of huge continuous masses of living matter of enormous extent, is most fanciful and improbable. It is opposed to well ascertained facts. So far from living matter growing to form very large collections, it divides in almost all known instances before it reaches the diameter even of $\frac{1}{500}$ of an inch. I think that the phenomena essential to living matter are only possible in minute masses separated from one another, so that each may be supplied with nutrient materials. *See* "Of Life," p. 64.

débris of living organisms which have passed away. Numerous minute living forms are, however, still found on it.

Dr. Wallich is of opinion that each coccosphere is just as much an independent structure at *Thalassicolla* or *Collosphœra,* and that, as in other cases, "nutrition is effected by a vital act," which enables the organism to extract from the surrounding medium the elements adapted for its nutrition. These are at length converted into its sarcode and shell material. In fact, in these lowest simplest forms, we find evidence of the working of an inherent vital power, and in them nutrition seems to be conducted upon the same principles as in the highest and most complex beings. In all cases the process involves, besides physical and chemical changes, purely *vital actions,* which cannot be imitated, and which cannot be explained by Physics and Chemistry.

Chemistry of Protoplasm.

From what has been said already, it must be obvious that the chemistry of the complex matter now termed protoplasm, embraces, 1, the chemistry of the formed matter, and 2, the chemistry of the active, living, growing, matter, of the organism. By chemical analysis we can ascertain the composition of the first, and can learn many facts concerning its elementary chemical characters ; but it is obvious that chemistry can teach us little with regard to the composition of the living matter, for we kill it when we attempt to analyze it; and in truth we analyze not the *living matter,* but the substances resulting from its death. Of course any one may say that the inanimate substances he obtains were the actual things of which the living matter was composed, but it is a mere assertion, for the bodies in question cannot be detected in the matter *while it is actually alive;* and when obtained they do not possess the properties or powers characteristic of the living matter. What, therefore, can be gained by asserting that these things constitute living matter? What is the use of trying to make people believe and confess that there is no difference between a living thing and the same thing dead, when it is clearly possible that there may be the very greatest difference?

And I must not omit to notice here a remark made by Mr. Herbert Spencer, which illustrates the extraordinary opinion entertained by him concerning the difference between living, growing, active, matter, and perfectly lifeless matter. "On the other hand (he says) the microscope has traced down organisms to simpler and simpler forms, until, in the *Protogenes* of Professor Hæckel there has been reached a type *distinguishable from a fragment of albumen only by its finely granular character.*"* Mr. Herbert Spencer should prepare a solution of albumen and a solution of "protogenes," and by careful evaporation he might obtain two extracts not distinguishable from one another. Both would exhibit a "finely granular character," and thus the important fact that there was no difference whatever between the inanimate albumen and the inanimate "protogenes" would be demonstrated. And as every one is now prepared to admit that there is no difference between dead "protogenes" and living "protogenes," we must of course accept the conclusion that the lowest forms of life are but forms of albumen. In this way "the chasm between the inorganic and the organic is being filled up!"

* 'The Principles of Psychology,' p. 137.

Notwithstanding the clever and subtle arguments which have been advanced in its favour, and repeated over and over again in almost every possible form, the new doctrine of life has exerted very little influence. It is absurd to expect that thoughtful persons will be convinced that vital phenonema are physical and chemical phenomena, simply by an authoritative assertion that they are so; and no matter how energetically the doctrine may be advocated, it will not be received unless it is proved to be founded upon facts. In spite of all that has been said, the chemist has taught us little concerning the nature of the changes which take place when pabulum becomes totally changed and converted into living matter, or when the latter gives rise to some peculiar kind of formed matter. He has shown us, it is true, that certain substances resulting in the organism during the disintegration of formed matter may be prepared artificially in the laboratory; but he knows as well as the physiologist, that their formation in the organism is conducted upon totally different principles, of the nature of which all are entirely ignorant. And it is childish to attempt, as some have done, to hide our ignorance by referring the actions to subtle influences, cell-laboratories, and molecular machinery, when every one knows there is nothing like a laboratory or machinery in any cell in any organism.

" Properties" of Matter.

Here are some specimens of the dogmatic assertions which have been advanced in place of facts and arguments in favour of the physico-chemical doctrines. "The difference between a crystal of calc spar and amorphous carbonate of lime corresponds to the difference between living matter and the matter which results from its death. Just as by chemical analysis we learn the composition of calc spar, so by chemical analysis we ascertain the composition of living matter. It is not probable that there is any real difference in the nature of the molecular forces which compel the carbonate of lime to assume and retain the crystalline form, and those which cause the albuminoid matter to move and grow, select and form and maintain its particles in a state of incessant motion. The property of crystallising is to crystallisable matter what the vital property is to albuminoid matter (protoplasm). The crystalline form corresponds to the organic form, and its internal structure to tissue structure. Crystalline force being a property of matter, vital force is but a property of matter." It might be objected that crystalline force keeps particles still and compels them to assume a constant form, while vital force prevents them from assuming any definite form at all and keeps them moving,—*form* being assumed only when the matter is withdrawn from the influence of the vital force ; but these and any other objections raised to the physical theory of life are accounted absurd and frivolous. It has been asserted positively that there is but one true theory of life—the physical theory. Its advocates seem to think that any objections raised to this ought not to be listened to, because they assert prophetically that by the rapid advance of molecular physics, the truth of their theory will *some day* be fully established.

The properties possessed by inorganic compounds are supposed to be due in some way to the properties of the elements of which they consist. Thus it has been remarked that the properties of water result from the properties of its constituent gases, and are not due to "aquosity," as if any reasonable man would think of referring the properties of water to such a "subtle influence" as "aquosity." It has been argued that since the properties of water are due to its gases and not to *aquosity*, the properties of protoplasm are due to its elements, Oxygen, Hydrogen, Nitrogen, and Carbon, and not to *vitality*. But the cases are by no means parallel. Of water there is but one kind.* Of protoplasm there are kinds innumerable. The constituent elements of the same particle of water may be separated and recombined again and again as many times as we please; but the elements of protoplasm once separated from one another, can never be combined again to form any kind of protoplasm. But further, every kind of protoplasm differs from every other kind most remarkably in the results of its living, one producing man, another dog, a third butterfly, a fourth amœba, and so on. Now, what can be more absurd than to suggest that the properties of man, dog, butterfly, and amœba are due not to vitality, but

---

* A hostile critic has discovered that there are at least two kinds, dirty water and clean water !

to the constituent elements of their tissues? Do the pro-perties of the elements of dog differ sufficiently from those of the elements of man, to account for the differences between dog and man. Have we not rather *identity of composition* in the living matter, and marvellous difference in the results of the vital actions? How, then, can the differences be due to the ordinary properties of the elements? Wonderful properties have indeed to be discovered in connection with elements before we can refer the differences in property of living beings compounded of them to the properties of the elements themselves. The argument advanced against vitality, as far as it rests upon the non-existence of aquosity, is utterly worthless, and it is astonishing that any writer who gave his readers credit for moderate intelligence should have adduced it at all.

The different forms and properties of living beings can only be explained by supposing the influence of force different from ordinary forces acting upon the matter of which they are composed, or upon the existence of properties other than the inorganic properties transmitted or handed down from pre-existing matter having similar, though, perhaps, not identical properties. These *vital properties* seem to be superadded to matter temporarily, and are obviously not permanent endowments. The one class of properties remains permanently attached to the elements of matter; the other may be once removed, but can never be restored. The material properties belong to the matter, whether living or dead; but where are the vital properties in the dead material? If physicists and chemists would restore to life that which is dead, we should all believe in the doctrine

they teach.   So long as they tell us their investigations only
tend towards such a consummation, they must expect a few
to be wanting in faith.

Sheep, Lobster, and Human Protoplasm.

Mr. Huxley seems to maintain that protoplasm may be
killed and dried, roasted and boiled, or otherwise altered,
and yet remain protoplasm ; but his "protoplasm" is after all
only albuminoid or protein matter.* Huxley says lobster-
protoplasm may be converted into human protoplasm, and
the latter again turned into living lobster.   But the statement
is incorrect ; because, in the process of assimilation "protoplasm" is entirely disintegrated, and is not converted into
the new tissue in the form of protoplasm at all ; and he
must permit me to remark that sheep cannot be transubstantiated into man, even by "subtle influences," nor can
dead protoplasm be converted into living protoplasm, or a
dead sheep into a living man.   And what is gained by calling
the matter of dead roast mutton and of a living growing sheep
by the same name ?   If the last is the physical basis of *life* one
does not see how the first can be so too, unless roast mutton
and living sheep are identical ; but surely Mr. Huxley does
not really mean to assert this.

It is remarkable that Huxley himself, some sixteen years

---

* Mr. Huxley says "all protoplasm is proteinaceous ; or, as the
white or albumen of an egg is one of the commonest examples of a
nearly pure protein matter, we may say that all *living matter* is more or
less albuminoid."   If the white of an egg is living matter, why should
not its shell be so considered ?

ago, drew a distinction between living and non-living matter which he now, without any explanation, utterly ignores. He remarked that the stone, the gas, the crystal, had an *inertia*, and tended to remain as they were unless some external influence affected them ; but that living things were characterized by the very opposite tendencies. He referred also to " the faculty of pursuing their own course" and the " inherent law of change in living beings." In 1853, the same authority actually found fault with those who attempted to reduce life to " mere attractions and repulsions," and considered physiology " simply as a complex branch of mere physics." He also remarked that "vitality is a property inherent in *certain kinds* of matter."

To sum up in few words. The term protoplasm has been applied to the viscid nitrogenous substance within the primordial utricle of the vegetable cell and to the threads and filaments formed in this matter; to the primordial utricle itself; to this and the substances which it encloses ; and to all these things, together with the cellulose wall ; to the matter composing the sarcode of the foraminifera ; to that which constitutes the amœba, white blood-corpuscle, and other naked masses of germinal matter ; to the matter between the so-called nucleus and muscular tissue, and to the contractile matter itself; to everything which exhibits contractility ; to nerve-fibres, and to other structures possessing remarkable endowments ; to the soft matter within an elementary part, as a cell of epithelium ; to the hard external part of such a cell; to the entire epithelial cell.

Inanimate albuminous matter has been regarded as protoplasm. Living things have been spoken of as masses of protoplasm; the same things dead have been said to be protoplasm. If the matter be boiled or roasted, it is still protoplasm; and there seems no reason why it should not be dissolved, and yet retain its name protoplasm.

GERMINAL OR LIVING MATTER, AND FORMED MATTER.

OTHING that lives is alive in every part. Probably no one would maintain that the shell of an oyster or mussel, for example, was, like the living moving mollusk itself, in a living state. Nevertheless, the shell *grows*, but upon careful examination it will be found that *growth* is restricted to certain points. It grows at the free edge and upon the inner surface, and thus increases in dimensions. By far the greater part of the shell, therefore, is as lifeless while it yet remains connected with the living animal as after it has been preserved in our cabinet. The new matter which is added to it by the living creature is prepared and formed through the instrumentality of living matter. In man, and the higher animals, the free portions of the nails and hair, the outer part of the cuticle, and a portion of the dental tissues, are evidently lifeless. But the waste and removal of these is compensated for to a great extent by the addition of new matter by living particles. Of the internal tissues a great part is also in a non-living condition, and it therefore becomes necessary in all inquiries concerning the nature of the changes and actions taking place in living beings, to determine at the outset, what parts of these beings are in a living state, and what parts have already ceased to live, although they may perform important service of a passive kind, and be connected with the matter that is actually alive. Even in the smallest organisms which exhibit the simplest characters, as well as in every texture of the most highly complex beings, we can demonstrate two kinds of matter, differing in most remarkable particulars from one another; or perhaps it would be more correct to say, matter in two *different states manifesting different properties* and exhibiting differences in appearance, chemical composition, &c., and physical characters. This distinction is essential and invariable, and although by calling everything entering into the composition of a living being by the same name, all differences of state, structure, and composition may be ignored, these cannot be destroyed; and every one who really desires to learn anything about the structure, growth, and actions of living things will find himself compelled to admit these differences, and will at once proceed to investigate how they are to be accounted for.

In my lectures at the Royal College of Physicians, in the spring of 1860, I demonstrated in various tissues of plants, animals, and man in health and disease, matter in the two different states above referred to, and I showed that every normal and abnormal cell or elemental unit of every tissue capable of growth, or possessing formative power, invariably consisted of matter in these states or conditions: 1. Living, active, formative; 2. Lifeless, passive, formed. In my preparations these were at once distinguished, the first being artificially coloured with carmine, while the matter in the last condition was unchanged.

As investigation proceeded, I became more and more

convinced of the importance of this distinction, and it was proved that the matter coloured, which had been considered by many authors to be of little importance, was really in the living, active, growing state. Upon it all growth, multi-plication, conversion, formation, and in short life depends. And in many instances when death occurred, the matter in the first state alone changed, while the last remained un-altered. The first was alone capable of dying, for, in fact, this only had been alive. On the other hand, the matter in the second condition, although it may possess very re-markable properties, and have a highly complex chemical composition never *grows* or *multiplies.* It never *converts* or *forms.* New matter *may be added* to it, but it cannot con-vert matter of itself. In short it does not live.

Lastly, facts and arguments were advanced which showed that all matter in the last or formed state was once in the first or living state, so that the properties it acquired and the characters it possessed as formed matter were to be attributed to the changes which had been brought about while the matter existed in the antecedent or living state.

There is reason to think that not even the smallest living particle seen under the 1–50th of an inch objective consists of matter in the same state in every part, for it consists of—1, living matter; 2, matter formed from this; and 3, pabulum, which 1 takes up.

The matter in the first state is alone concerned in *develop-ment, and the production of those materials which ultimately take the form of tissue, secretion, deposit, as the case may be.* It alone possesses the power of growth and of producing matter like itself out of materials differing from it entirely

D

in properties and powers. I therefore called it *germinal* or *living matter*, to distinguish it from the *formed material*, which is in all cases destitute of these properties. The difference between germinal or living matter and the pabulum which nourishes it, on the one hand, and the formed material which is produced by it, on the other, is, I believe, absolute. The pabulum does not shade by imperceptible gradations into the living matter, and this latter into the formed material; but the transition from one state into the other is sudden and abrupt, although there may be much living matter mixed with a little lifeless matter or *vice versâ*. The ultimate particles of matter pass from the lifeless into the living state, and from the latter into the dead state, suddenly. Matter cannot be said to *half-live* or *half-die*. It is either *dead* or *living*, *animate* or *inanimate;* and formed matter has ceased to live.

Matter may be more or less perfectly or imperfectly formed, and formed matter may differ in hardness, colour, consistence, and a number of other qualities, and it may gradually pass from one state into the other; but nothing of this kind is observed in the case of the germinal matter. The formed matter may possess very remarkable properties, and may undergo various physical and chemical changes under the influence of heat, moisture, oxygen, &c. It may permit some fluids to permeate it, and may interfere with the passage of others. It may contribute to the stability of the organism, and perform a variety of important functions, but it cannot take the place of the germinal or living matter, nor in many cases does it exhibit its characteristic properties after the death of the germinal matter belonging to it.

The terms Living Matter, Formed Matter, and Pabulum.

Since many kinds of formed matter had been called *protoplasm* as well as the matter which is in the living state, I should have been wrong if I had employed that term in speaking of *living matter.* From the time when my researches were made to the present, the confusion in the use of the word protoplasm has increased, until every form of tissue has been thus called, as well as every kind of germinal or living matter. And it would only add to the existing confusion if any attempt were now made again to alter the meaning of the word; so that, upon the whole, it seems better to use the more simple term *living or germinal matter* to denote the growing, active, moving substance which is peculiar to everything living, and which is alone concerned in the multiplication, growth, and formation of all tissues and organisms.

Living or germinal matter, formed matter, and *pabulum,* are the only terms required in describing the development, formation, and growth of any tissue, the production of secretions, and other phenomena peculiar to living things; and I have ventured to suggest the use of these terms, because they have the advantage of being simple. They can be accurately defined and distinguished from other terms. They are short, expressive, and can be remembered without difficulty, and there is certainly an absence of that mysteriousness which hangs about so many of our scientific words in ordinary use, and greatly adds to the difficulties experienced by the student.

General Characters of Germinal Matter.

The characters of germinal matter may be studied in the lowest organisms in existence, and in plants, as well as in man and the higher animals. Germinal or living matter is always transparent, colourless, and, as far as can be ascertained by examination with the highest powers, perfectly structureless, and it exhibits these same characters at every period of existence. The germinal matter of the thallus of the growing sugar fungus exists in considerable quantity, and is well adapted for examination. The growing extremity of the branch is rounded, and here the process of growth is going on with great activity. When the operation of staining has been conducted successfully, these growing extremities are more deeply stained than the rest of the germinal matter. A similar fact is observed if one of the placental tufts is submitted to examination. At the extreme end of each tuft is a mass of germinal matter which is darkly stained by the carmine fluid. Behind this, and growing towards it, is the vascular loop; but as the tufts grow, the mass of formless, structureless germinal matter at the end of each moves onwards, the vessels being developed in its wake. This formless living matter moves forwards nd burrows, as it were, into the nutrient pabulum, some of which it takes up as it moves on. It is not pushed from behind, but it moves forward of its own accord. In a similar manner the advancing fungus bores its way into the material upon which it feeds, and the root filament insinuates itself into interstices between the particles of the soil. In the hair, the germinal matter grows and multiplies at the base or bulb, pushing the firm and already formed tissue before it. In the first case, the germinal matter is increasing at the extremity of a filament which it spins behind it as it moves on ; in the last, the tissue already formed is *pushed on* by the production of new texture in its rear. The extremity of the hair is its oldest part, and nearest to the root is the tissue which was most recently formed. But whether germinal matter moves on in its entirety, or, advancing from a fixed point, forms a filament, a tube, or other structure which accumulates behind it, or itself remains stationary while the products of formation are forced onwards in one direction, or outwards in all, the nature of the force exerted is the same, and due to the *marvellous power which one part of a living mass possesses of moving in advance of another portion of the same, as may be actually seen to occur in the humble amœba, in the mucus- or in the white blood-corpuscle from man's organism, as well as in the pus corpuscle formed in disease.*

Amœba.—Among the simplest living things known to us are the amœbæ, which might be almost described as animate masses of perfectly transparent moving matter. Amœbæ, fig. 4, pl. II., can be obtained for examination by placing a small fragment of animal or vegetable matter in a little water in a wine-glass, and leaving it in the light part of a warm room for a few days. I have found it convenient to introduce a few filaments of cotton wool into the water. The amœbæ collect amongst the fibres, which prevent them from being crushed by the pressure of the thin glass cover.

The delicate material of which these simple creatures are composed exhibits no indications of actual structure,

although it is darker and more granular in some parts than
in others. The germinal matter of all organisms, and of
the tissues and organs of each organism, exhibits precisely
the same characters. It *lives*, and *grows*, and *forms* in the
same way, although the conditions under which the phenomena of life growth and formation are carried on differ
very much in different kinds of germinal matter. A tem-
perature at which one kind will live and grow actively will
be fatal to many other kinds. So, too, as regards pabulum,
—substances which are appropriated by one form of ger
minal matter will act as a poison to another. But the way
in which the germinal matter moves, divides and subdivides,
grows, and undergoes conversion into tissue, is the same in
all. Many remarkable differences in structure, properties,
action, and character, are associated with close similarity,
if not actual identity of composition. These must, there
fore, be attributed not to properties of elements, physical
forces, chemical affinities, or other characters which we
can ascertain or estimate by physical examination, but to
a difference in *vital power* which is inherited, which we
cannot estimate, but which it would be unreasonable to
ignore.

On Vital Movements.

One characteristic of every kind of living matter is
spontaneous movement. This, unlike the movement of
any kind of non-living matter yet discovered, occurs in all
directions, and seems to depend upon changes in the matter
itself, rather than upon impulses communicated to the particles from without.

I have been able to watch the movements of small amœbæ, which multiplied freely without first reaching the size of the ordinary individuals. I have represented the appearance under a magnifying power of 5,000 diameters of some of the most minute amœbæ I have been able to discover. (Plate II, fig. 3.) Several of these were less than $\frac{1}{1000000}$th of an inch in diameter, and yet were in a state of most active movement. The alteration in form was very rapid, and the different tints in the different parts of the moving mass, resulting from alterations in thickness, were most distinctly observed. The living bodies might, in fact, be described as consisting of minute portions of very transparent material, exhibiting the most active movements in various directions, in every part, and capable of absorbing nutrient materials from the surrounding medium. A portion which was at one moment at the lowest point of the mass would pass in an instant to the highest part. In these movements one part seemed, as it were, to pass through other parts, while the whole mass moved now in one, now in another direction, and movements in different parts of the mass occurred in directions different from that in which the whole was moving. What movements in lifeless matter can be compared with these?

The movements above described continue as long as the external conditions remain favourable; but, if these alter and the amœba be exposed to the influence of unfavourable circumstances—as altered pabulum, cold, &c.—the movements become very slow, and then completely stop. The organism becomes spherical, and the trace of soft formed material upon the surface increases until a firm protective covering, envelope, or cell-wall results. In this way the life of the germinal matter is preserved until the return of favourable conditions, when the living matter emerges from its prison, grows, and soon gives rise to a colony of new amœbæ, which exhibit the characteristic movements.

Mucus Corpuscle.—Every one knows that upon the surface of the mucous membrane of the air-passages, even in health, there is a small quantity of a soft viscid matter generally termed *mucus.* This mucus, said to be *secreted* by the mucous membrane, contains certain oval or spherical bodies or corpuscles, which are transparent and granular. From the changes of form which take place in them, it is certain that the matter of which they are composed is almost diffluent. These corpuscles or cells are *mucous corpuscles*, but they have no cell-wall. They are separated from each other by, and are embedded in, a more or less transparent, viscid, tenacious substance formed by the corpuscles, and termed *mucus.* (Plate II, fig. 1.)

No language could convey a correct idea of the changes which may be seen to take place in the form of the living mucus or pus corpuscle; every part of the substance of a corpuscle exhibits distinct alterations within a few seconds. The material which was in one part may move to another part. Not only does the position of the component particles alter with respect to one another, but it never remains the same. There is no *alternation* of movements. Were it possible to take hundreds of photographs at the briefest intervals, no two would be exactly alike, nor would they exhibit different gradations of the same change; nor is it possible to represent the movements with any degree of accuracy by drawings, because the outline is changing in many parts at the same moment. I have seen an entire corpuscle move onwards in one definite direction for a distance equal to its own length or more. Protrusions would occur principally at one end, and the general mass would gradually follow. Again, protrusions would take place in the same direction, and slowly the remainder of the corpuscle would be drawn onwards, until the whole had been removed from the place it originally occupied, and would advance onward for a short distance in the mucus in which it was embedded. From the first protrusions smaller protrusions very often occur, and these gradually become pear-shaped, remaining attached by a narrow stem, and in a few seconds perhaps again become absorbed into the general mass. From time to time, however, some of the small spherical portions are detached from the parent mass, and become independent masses of germinal matter, which grow until they become ordinary mucus corpuscles, pl. II, fig. 2. Are these phenomena, I would ask, at all like any known to occur in lifeless material?

The component particles evidently alter their positions in a most remarkable manner. One particle may move in advance of another, or round another. A portion may move into or round another portion. A bulging may occur at one point of the circumference, or at ten or twenty different points at the same moment. The moving power evidently resides in every particle of a very transparent, invariably colourless, and structureless material. By the very highest powers only an indication of minute spherical particles can be discerned. Because molecules have been seen in some of the masses of moving matter, the motion has been attributed to these. It is true the molecules do move, but the living transparent material in which they are situated *moves first*, and the molecules flow into the extended portion. The movements cannot, therefore, be ordinary *molecular movements*. It has been said that the movements may result from diffusion, but what diffusion or other movement with which we are acquainted at all resembles these? Observers have ascribed them to a difference in density of different parts, but who has been able to produce such movements by preparing fluids of different density? But further, in the case of the living matter, these supposed fluids of different density make themselves and retain their differences in density.

Nor is it any explanation of the movements to attribute them to inherent " irritability," unless we can show in what this *irritability* essentially consists. Some dismiss the matter by saying that the movements depend upon the property of " contractility," but the movements of germinal matter are totally distinct from contractility, as manifested by muscular tissue; since they take place in every direction, and every movement differs from the rest, while in muscular contraction there is a constant repetition of changes taking place alternately in directions at right angles to one another; and hence, if the movements in question be due to contractility, it is necessary to assume two very different kinds of contractile property.

The movements in the mucus corpuscle and in the *amœba*, are of the same nature as those which occur in the germinal matter of many plants, as is easily observed in the cells of the leaves of the vallisneria or the anacharis, in the chara

Fig. 1.

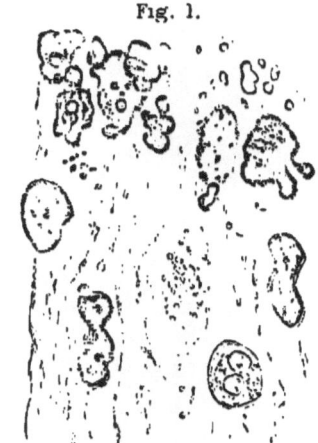

Fig. 2.

One of the living mucus corpuscles represented
in Fig. 1, magnified by the $\frac{1}{50} = 800$ diameters,
showing alterations in form during one
minute.

Mucus from the trachea during life, magnified
700 diameters.

Fig. 3.

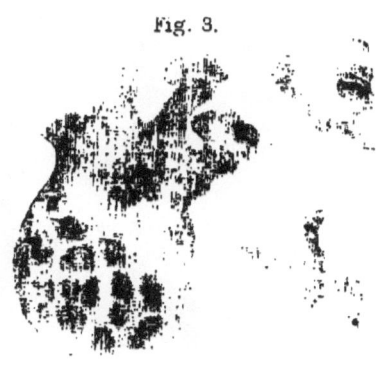

Very minute living amœbæ, magnified 2000
diameters.

Fig. 4.

Small amœba, magnified by the $\frac{1}{50} = 250$
diameters.

Fig. 5.

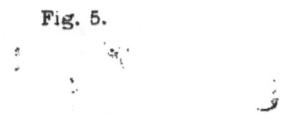

Minute particle of germinal matter from living
pus corpuscle, showing the different forms
which it assumed in the course of five seconds.
× 2800.

Fig. 6.

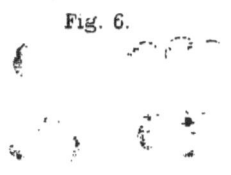

Particles of germinal matter from vaccine
lymph. × 1000.

1000th of an inch |_____| × 1000.

A line five times the length of this will represent the $\frac{1}{200}$ of an inch magnified 600.

and in the hairs of the flower of Tradescantia ; and the appearance of the living matter under very high powers is precisely the same in all cases. Similar movements certainly occur in pus, and in cancer, and probably in every kind of living matter in health and in disease, pl. II, figs. 5 and 6. In some instances the movements continue for many hours after the living matter has been removed from the surface upon which it grew. In other cases, and we shall not be surprised that this should be so in the higher animals, death occurs the instant the conditions under which the living matter exists are but slightly modified. In many instances no movements can be seen, but the evidence of their occurrence is almost as decided as if they were visible, for we discern certain results which can only be explained by the occurrence of such movements as have been referred to.

I have often tried to persuade the physicist, who has so long prophesied the existence of molecular machinery in living beings, to seek for it in the "colourless, structureless," germinal matter. But he contents himself with asserting that such machinery exists, although he cannot see it or make it evident to himself or others.

Of New Centres—Nuclei and Nucleoli.

In many masses of germinal matter a smaller spherical portion.often appearing a mere point.is observed, and in some cases this divides before the division of the parent mass takes places. This, however, is not necessary to the process, for division takes place in cases in which no such bodies are to be seen, and it frequently happens that one or more of these smaller spots or spherical masses may appear in its substance, *after* a portion of germinal matter has been detached from the parent mass. These are to be regarded as *new centres* composed of living matter. Within these a second series is sometimes produced. The first have been called *nuclei*, and those within them *nucleoli*. Marvellous powers have been attributed to nuclei and neucleoli, and by many these are supposed to be the agents alone concerned in the process of multiplication and reproduction. Nuclei and nucleoli are always more intensely coloured with alkaline colouring matters than other parts of the living or germinal matter, a fact which is alone sufficient to show the difference between a true nucleus or new centre, and an oil globule, which has often been wrongly termed a nucleolus. I have endeavoured to show that the bodies called nuclei and nucleoli may be regarded as new centres which have arisen in already existing germinal matter. These new centres may be few or very numerous, and there may be many successive series of such centres, each, when it comes to be developed, manifesting powers different from the pre-existing series. And in certain cases it would appear that as this process of formation of new centres, one within the other proceeds, new powers are acquired, or if we suppose that all possessed the same powers, those masses only which were last produced retain them, and manifest them when placed under favourable conditions. Although nuclei and nucleoli are germinal or living matter, they are not undergoing conversion into formed material. Under certain conditions the nucleus may increase, and exhibit all the phenomena of ordinary germinal matter—new nuclei may be developed within it, new nucleoli within them; so that ordinary germinal matter may become formed material, its nucleus growing larger and taking its place." The original nucleolus now becomes the nucleus, and new nucleoli make their appearance in what was the original nucleolus. The whole process consists of evolution from centres, and the production of new centres within pre-existing centres. Zones of colour, of different intensity, are often observed in a cell coloured with carmine ; the outermost or oldest, or that part which is losing its vital powers, and becoming converted into formed material, being very slightly coloured,—the most central part, or the nucleus, *although furthest from the colouring solution*, exhibiting the greatest intensity of colour. These points are illustrated in Pl. VI, fig. 19, and some other figures.

Germinal matter, in a comparatively quiescent state is not unfrequently entirely destitute of nuclei, but these bodies sometimes make their appearance if the mass be more freely supplied with nutrient matter. This fact may be noticed in the case of the connective tissue corpuscles, and the masses of germinal matter connected with the walls of vessels, nerves, muscular tissue, epithelium, &c., which often exhibit no nuclei (or according to some, nucleoli), but soon after these tissues become supplied with an increased quantity of pabulum, several small nuclei make their appearance in all parts of the germinal matter. (Pl. VIII, fig. 36.)

So far from nuclei being formed *first* and the other elements of the cell *deposited around them*, they make their appearance in the substance of a pre-existing mass of germinal matter, as has been already stated. The true nucleus and nucleolus are not composed of special constituents differing from the germinal matter, nor do they perform any special operations. Small oil-globules, which invariably result from post-mortem changes in any germinal matter, have often been mistaken for nuclei and nucleoli, but these terms if employed at all should be restricted to the minute masses of germinal matter referred to.

The Cell or Elementary Part.

The living matter, with the formed matter upon its surface, whatever may be the structure, properties, and consistence of the latter, is *the anatomical unit, the elementary part or cell.* This may form the entire organism, in which case, it must be regarded as a complete individual. Millions of such elementary parts or cells are combined to form every tissue and organ of man and the higher animals. However much organisms and tissues in their fully formed state may vary as regards the character, properties, and composition of the formed material, all were first in the condition of *clear, transparent, structureless, formless* living matter.

Every *growing* cell, and every cell *capable of growth*, contains *germinal matter.* The young cell seems to consist almost entirely of this living material—a fact well observed in a specimen of cuticle from the young frog, which may be contrasted with more advanced cuticle from the same animal. In the mature cells only a small mass of germinal matter (usually termed the nucleus) remains.

In the fully formed fat cell there is so little germinal

PLATE III.

OVA OF THE COMMON STICKLEBACK.
PRODUCTION OF NEW LIVING CENTRES IN PRE-EXISTING LIVING MATTER.

Fig. 7.

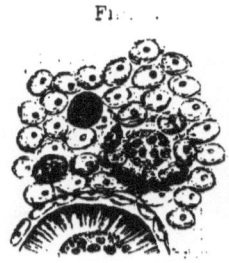

A portion of ovarian ova undergoing development, in the midst of a delicate tissue composed of cells. Magnified 60 diameters.

Fig. 8.

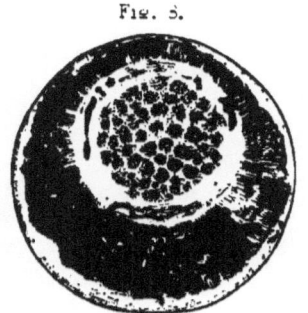

Ovarian ovum, with large germinal vesicle. The yolk cracked and exhibiting fissures radiating outwards. Magnified 100 diameters

Fig. 9.

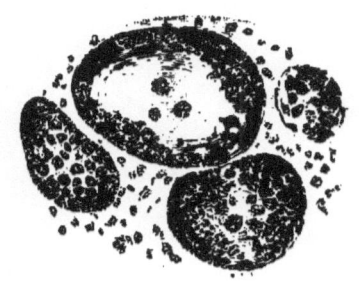

Germinal spots from a ruptured germinal vesicle. × 550. The ovum was 1/27 inch in diameter, and the germinal vesicle 1/130.

Fig. 10.

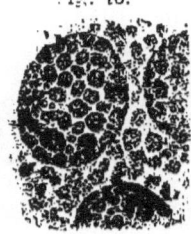

Two of the small germinal spots, with new centres within them. × 700

Fig. 11.

Germinal spots, with new centres (nuclei) within them, and more minute germinal spots in the intervals between them. × 550.

× 550.

matter left, that it may be easily be overlooked. In disease, on the other hand, the germinal matter may increase to three or four times its ordinary dimensions, when it becomes a very striking object. The ovum at an early period of its development is but a cell consisting of a mass of germinal matter, with a new centre and often with numerous new centres (known as germinal spots or nuclei) embedded in it, enclosed in a capsule of formed material.

The mode of formation of the cell, or elemental unit, as well as the origin from it of other units is well illustrated in the formation of the ovum. In pl. III, fig 7, the cells constituting the tissue of the ovary of the common stickle-back are represented, and amongst them are seen true ova at a very early period of development. The youngest of these differs but little from the cells amongst which it lies. It is, in fact, but one of these which has advanced in development beyond the rest. In fig. 8, a small but complete ovum is seen with its germinal, or living matter, here called germinal vesicle, surrounded by the yolk which consists of formed matter. In the germinal matter are seen numerous germinal spots, which are new living centres of growth originating in living matter. In these are new centres, figs. 9, 10, 11, and in these last others would have appeared at a later period. In all cases the lifeless nutrient material must pass into the very centre of the living particles, before the peculiar *vital* properties are communicated to it.

On the Production of Formed Material.

The processes of growth and increase, as they occur in the tissues of all fully-formed living beings, may be well studied in the simple tissue which forms the external covering of the body, and is prolonged in a modified form into the internal cavities. If a thin section be made perpendicularly through this, down to the tissue which contains the nerves and blood-vessels upon which it rests, the appearances represented in pl. IV, fig. 12 will be observed.

In the first place, it will be remarked that in equal bulks of the tissue there is a larger quantity of germinal matter in the lower part, *a*, which is close to the vessels, than in the upper part, *c*, which is a long distance from the nutrient surface, and that the converse is the case as regards the formed material which gives to this tissue its properties and physical characters. Secondly, it will be noticed that the individual masses of germinal matter increase in size till they arrive at about half way towards the surface, *b*, while from this point to the surface they diminish, *c;* and thirdly, that the distance between them increases on account of the increased formation and accumulation of formed material. By the time the cells have reached the surface, the distance between the masses of germinal matter is reduced again, by the drying and condensation of the formed material.

The changes which each individual cell or anatomical unit passes through may now be considered. At the deep aspect near the nutrient surface are masses of germinal matter embedded in a soft, mucus-like, and, as yet, continuous

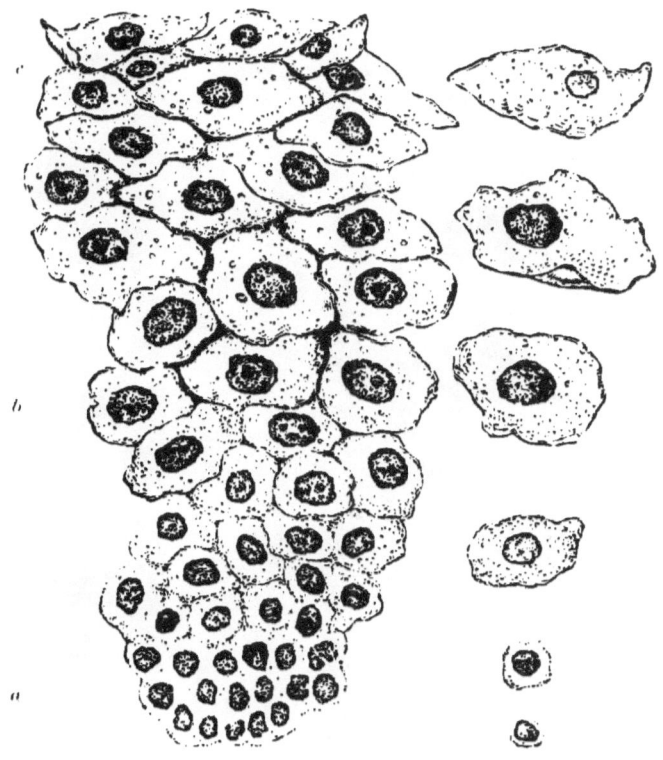

formed material, *a.* The masses of germinal matter divide, and each of the resulting masses becomes invested with a thin layer of the mucus-like matter. In this way, the elementary parts or cells multiply in number, to compensate for the loss of those old cells which are gradually removed from the surface.* Each mass of germinal matter increases in size by the absorption of nutrient pabulum, which, as in all other cases, passes through the layer of formed material. But at the same time, a portion of the germinal matter undergoes conversion into formed material, which accumulates upon the surface within that already formed, and as each new layer is deposited upon the surface of the germinal matter, those layers of formed material already produced are stretched, and with them the last developed are more or less incorporated. Pl. VIII, fig. 28, p. 60. For a time, the germinal matter increases, while new-formed material is being produced. In other words, both the constituent parts of the entire cell increase in amount up to a certain period of its life. Pl. IV *b.* But as new cells continue to be produced below, those already formed are gradually removed farther and farther from the vascular surface, while at the same time their formed material becomes more condensed and less permeable to nutrient matter. From this point, each entire cell ceases to increase in size, while the germinal matter actually

* The description here given is not strictly accurate, inasmuch as the new masses of germinal matter do not *all* move in a direction *towards* the surface. Some tend in the opposite direction, towards the subcuticular tissue, but this need not be discussed here, as it would complicate the description without helping in any way to elucidate the question now being considered.

E

diminishes, because it undergoes conversion into formed material; at the same time, owing to the increased density of the formed material, and its greater distance from the vessels, little new pabulum is taken up to compensate for this. The germinal matter (nucleus) becomes smaller as the cell advances in age. So that it is possible to judge of the age of a cell, irrespective of its size, by the relative amount of its component substances. In old cells, there is much formed material in proportion to the germinal matter, while young cells seem to be composed almost entirely of the latter substance. In very old cells, the small portion of germinal matter still unconverted into formed material, dies, and the cell having by this time arrived at the surface, is cast off,—a mass of perfectly passive, lifeless, formed material.

The facts here described are illustrated in the figure represented in Pl. IV, which should be carefully studied.

Of the so-called Intercellular Substance.

In cartilage and some other tissues, there is no line of separation between the portion of formed material which belongs to each mass of germinal matter, as is the case in epithelium, but the formed material throughout the entire tissue forms an uninterrupted mass of tissue, matrix, or, as it has been termed, connective substance. Pl. V. From the apparent essential difference in structure, it has been supposed that tissues of this character were developed upon a principle very different to that upon which epithelial structures were produced. It has been maintained by some that in cartilage a cell wall, distinct from the intervening transparent material, existed around each cell, and it has

EPITHELIAL CELLS AND CARTILAGE, SHOWING FORMED MATERIAL IN THE TWO TISSUES RESPECTIVELY AND THE MODE OF ITS FORMATION.

Fig. 13.

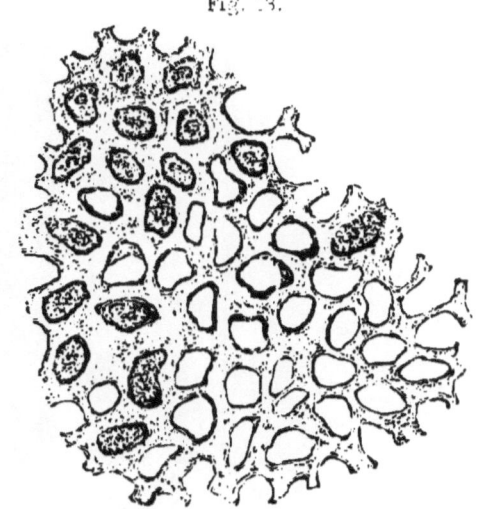

Fig. 14.

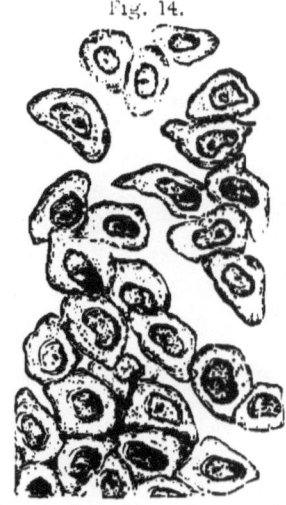

Superficial and middle layers of the conjunctiva (or mucous membrane covering the front of the eye) of a calf showing the formed material, continuous and not yet separated into separate masses or nuclei, with masses of nuclei rather. Beneath are the separate cells. ×350.

Superficial or outer cells, from the same specimen as Fig. 13, showing formed material belonging to each mass of germinal matter, giving rise to the appearance of separate cells. ×350.

Fig.

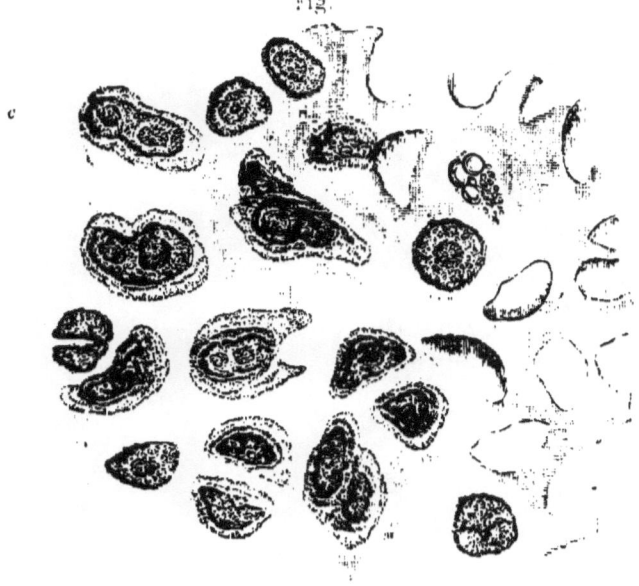

been very generally concluded that the matrix was deposited between the cells, and hence this was called "*intercellular substance.*" But it must not be supposed that epithelium is in all cases to be distinguished from cartilage by the existence of separate cells. In many forms of epithelium at an early period of formation, the formed material corresponding to the several masses of germinal matter is continuous throughout, and presents no indications of division into separate cells. This is well seen in the lower part of the specimen represented in pl. IV, but in fig. 13, pl. V, an unusually striking example of this is given. The specimen was taken from the deeper portion of the conjunctival epithelium of man. Not only is there no indication of division into distinct cells, but the structure would be described as a matrix exhibiting spaces occupied by the masses of germinal matter. The arrangement exactly corresponds with that existing in the case of cartilage, and the masses of germinal matter with a thin investment of formed material may be removed just as in that tissue. It is, therefore, clearly erroneous to consider cartilage and epithelium as representatives of different *classes* of tissues. The analogy between them will be at once understood by a glance at fig. 13, and fig. 15, which have been carefully copied from actual specimens. In fig. 14, a portion of older epithelium from the same surface is represented. In this, each mass of germinal matter is invested with its own layers of formed material, and these are distinct from neighbouring portions. A "cell," or elementary part of fully-formed cartilage and tendon, consists of a mass of germinal matter, with a proportion of formed material around it. A line passing midway between the several masses of germinal matter would mark roughly the limit of the formed material, corresponding to each particular mass of germinal matter, and this would correspond with the outer part of the surface or boundary of the epithelial cell.

In order to understand the true relation of the so-called intercellular substance of cartilage or tendon to the masses of germinal matter, it is necessary to study the tissue at different ages. At an early period of development, these tissues appear to consist of masses of germinal matter only. As development advances, the formed material increases, and the masses of germinal matter become separated farther and farther from one another. Pl. VI, fig. 16. The appearances of a cell wall around the germinal matter in the fully-formed tissue, and other alterations which occur, and anomalous appearances which often result as age advances, can be even more readily understood upon the view here advanced, than upon the intercellular-substance theory which has been so strongly supported by some observers. *See* pl. VI, figs. 16 to 22.

Of the Formation of the Contractile Tissue of Muscle.

A muscle " cell," or elementary part, will consist, like that of cartilage and tendon, of the so-called nucleus, with a portion of the muscular tissue corresponding to it. In general arrangement it closely resembles what is seen in tendon. The contractile material of muscle may be shown to be continuous with the germinal matter, and oftentimes a thin filament of the transversely striated tissue may be detached with the oval mass of germinal matter still con-

Fig. 16.

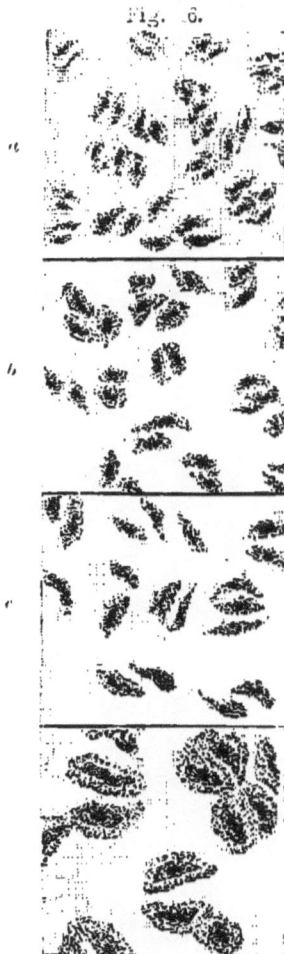

a

b

c

Cartilage at different ages. a, kitten at birth; b, six weeks old & nearly full grown; d a b cat. × 215. Showing alteration in the relative proportions of germinal matter and formed material at different ages.

Fig. 17.

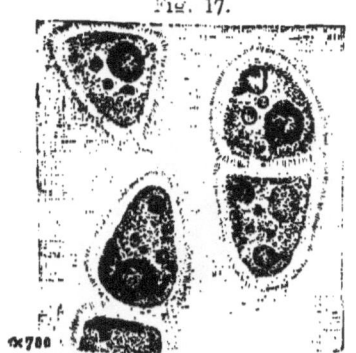

×700

Cartilage cells, showing germinal matter and formed material. × 70.

Fig. 18.

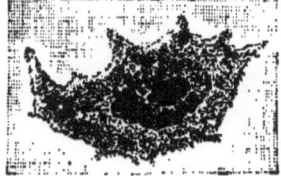

Young cartilage, kitten, showing the GROWTH OF THE GERMINAL MATTER WITH FORMED MATERIAL IN WHICH IT IS UNDERGOING CONVERSION. × 1800.

Fig. 19.

Cartilage cells showing germinal matter about to undergo conversion into formed material.

Fig. 20.

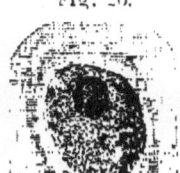

Fig. 21.

Fig. 22.

These figures show the actual conversion of the germinal matter of cartilage into the formed material of tissue. In b, and c, a piece of cartilage has been formed in the very centre of the germinal matter. Which is at once formed material and life, this, was at one time previously germinal matter and living. × 500.

BOTH OF ABOUT   × 700.

nected with it, showing that, as in tendon, the germinal matter passes uninterruptedly into the formed material. In the formation of the contractile tissue, the germinal matter seems to move onwards, and at its posterior part gradually undergoes conversion into tissue. At the same time it absorbs nutrient material, and thus, although a vast amount of contractile tissue may have been produced, the germinal matter which formed it may not have altered in bulk. Pl. VII, fig. 25. The fibres of yellow elastic tissue are formed in the same manner, and each fibre is thickened by the formation of new material from germinal matter, which lies upon the external surface of each fibre, fig. 26.

The Formation of Nerve Fibres.

The nerve fibre is composed of formed material, which is structurally continuous with the formed material of the nerve cells of the nerve centres. A nerve fibre at an early period of development consists of a number of oval masses of germinal matter linearly arranged. As development proceeds, these become separated farther and farther from one another, and the *tissue* which is thus spun off as they become separated, is the nerve. Pl. VII, fig. 27.

What is essential to the Cell?

All that is essential to the cell or elementary part is *matter that is in the living* state—*germinal matter*, and matter that *has been in the living state—formed material*. With these is usually associated a certain proportion of matter about to become living—the pabulum or food. So that we may say that in every living thing we have matter in three different states—matter about to become living, matter actually living, and matter that has lived. The last, like the first, is non-living, but unlike this it *has been* in the living state, and has had impressed upon it certain characters which it could not have acquired in any other way. By these characters we know that it has lived, for we can no more cause matter artificially to exhibit the characters of the dried leaf, the lifeless wood, shell, bone, hair, or other tissue, than we can make living matter itself in our laboratories.

Cells are not like Bricks in a Wall.

Cells forming a tissue have been compared to bricks in a wall, but the cells are not like bricks, they have not the same constitution in every part, nor are they made first and then embedded in the mortar. Each brick of the natural wall grows of itself, places itself in position, forms and embeds itself in the mortar of its own making. The whole wall grows in every part, and while growing may throw out bastions which grow and adapt themselves perfectly to the altering structure. Even now it is argued by some that because things, like fully formed cells, may be made artificially, the actual cells are formed in the same sort of way—an argument as forcible as would be that of a person, who after a visit to Madame Tussaud's exhibition, seriously maintained that our textures were constructed upon the same plan as the life-like wax figures he had seen there.

Every one who really studies the elementary parts of tissues and investigates the changes which occur as the germinal matter passes through various stages of change

until the fully developed structure results, will be careful
not to accept without due consideration the vague generali-
sations of those who persist in authoritatively declaring that
the changes occurring in cell growth are merely mechanical
and chemical, although they are unable to produce by any
means at their disposal a particle of fibrine, a piece of cartilage, or even a fragment of coral. They avoid the difficulty
as regards the germinal matter by ignoring its existence, and
attribute to a "molecular machinery" which the mind cannot
conceive, and which cannot be rendered evident to the
senses, all those wonderful phenomena which are really due
to vital power. Moreover, resemblances to living organisms
of the most fanciful kind are adduced apparently for the
purpose of leading people to believe that non-living matter
behaves like that which is alive.*

On the Nutrition of a Living Cell.

In nutrition, the active changes are exclusively confined
to the germinal matter. The formed material is passive,

---

* Professor Tyndall describes (*Proceedings of the Royal Society*,
vol. xvii, No. 105) the changes resulting from the influence of light on
the vapour of an aqueous solution of hydriodic acid. His rhapsodical
description, which extends over an entire page, contains the following
curious allusions and comparisons :—A cloud was developed like an
organism from a formless mass to a marvellously complex structure ;
spectral cones with filmy drapery ; exquisite vases with the faintest
clouds, like spectral sheets of liquid, falling over their edges ; clouds
like roses, tulips, sunflowers, and bottles one within the other ; a cloud
like a fish, with eyes, gills, and feelers, and like a jelly fish, with the
internal economy of a highly complex organism, exhibiting the twoness
of the animal form ; as perfect as if it had been turned in a lathe ; and
likely to prove exceedingly valuable to pattern designers !

and probably acts like a filter, permitting some things to pass and interfering with the passage of others. In nutrition, pabulum becomes germinal matter to compensate for the germinal matter which has been converted into formed material. Now let us consider the order of these changes, and endeavour to express them in the simplest possible manner.

Let the germinal matter which *came from pre-existing germinal matter* be called *a;* the non-living pabulum, some of the elements of which are about to be converted into germinal matter, shall be *b;* and the non-living formed material resulting from changes in the germinal matter, *c.*

It is to be remarked that *b* does not contain *c* in solution, neither can *c* be made out *b* unless *b* first passes through the condition *a,* and *a* cannot be formed artificially, but must come from pre-existing *a.*

In all cases *b* is transformed by *a* into *a,* and *a* undergoes conversion into *c.* Can anything be more unlike chemical and physical change? Neither *a,* nor *b,* nor *c* can be made by the chemist; nor if you give him *b* can he make *a* or *c* out of it; nor can he tell you anything about the "molecular condition" or chemical constitution of *a,* for the instant he commences his analysis *a* has ceased to be *a,* and he is merely dealing with products resulting from the death of *a,* not with the actual living *a* itself. The course which the pabulum takes in the nutrition of the germinal matter of a cell is represented by the arrows in fig. 23, pl. VII.

NUTRITION AND MOVEMENT OF GERMINAL MATTER

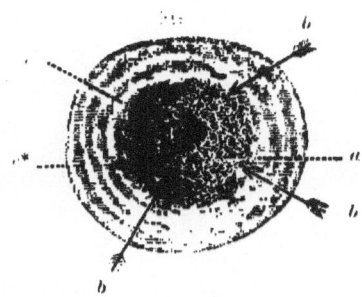

Fig.

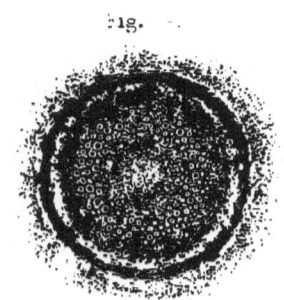

cell or elementary part. *a*, formed matter.
b, supposed path of moving matter in the direction
indicated by the arrows; these showing the formed
material and *a* passing into the germinal matter
b. Oldest formed material has produced
c oldest portion of formed matter.

a minute particle of germinal matter show
is composed of small particles of living matter
thin layer of newly formed material on su
formed of changes.

formed matter and formed material (contractile tissue) the passage the germinal matt
in the direction of the arrow. It is between *a* and *b*. It has been form
passes toward *b* thicker in the filament of contractile tissue the newest has been formed by

Fig.

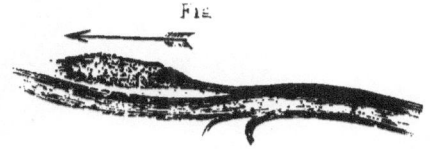

portion of a contractile tissue from in the limb constitution in a moving a
in contraction are rounded formed the yellow elastic tissue is its process. It has been said th
formed without the agency of germ cells, but a great number mass
germinal matter can be demonstrated in well-prepared specimens.

Fig.

development of young dark-bordered nerve fibres at a very early period, showing germin
matter and formed material of young elementary parts x about 50

Of the Increase of Cells.

Several distinct modes of cell increase or multiplication have been described, but in all cases the process depends upon the germinal matter only. It is this which divides ; and it is the only part of the cell which is actively concerned in the process of multiplication. It may divide into two or more equal portions, or give off many buds or offsets, each of which grows as a separate body as soon as it is detached. Pl. VIII.

The formed material of the cell is perfectly passive in the process of increase and multiplication. If soft or diffluent, a portion of this may collect around each of the masses into which the germinal matter has divided, but it does not grow or move in and form a partition, as has often been stated. When a septum or partition exists, it results not from "growing in," but it is simply produced by a portion of the germinal matter undergoing conversion into formed material of which the partition is composed. Pl. V, fig. 15 *a* and *b*.

Of the Changes in the Cell in Disease.

I have endeavoured to show that of the different constituents of the fully formed cell, the germinal matter is alone concerned in all active change. This is in fact the only portion of the cell which *lives*, while at an early period of development, some of the structures usually regarded as essential to cell existence are altogether absent, and the cell is but a mass of germinal matter. But it must be borne in mind that at all periods of life, in certain parts of the textures and organs, and in the nutrient fluids, are masses

of germinal matter, destitute of any cell-wall, and exactly
resembling those of which at an early period the embryo
is entirely composed.   White blood and lymph corpuscles,
chyle corpuscles, many of the corpuscles in the spleen,
thymus and thyroid, corpuscles in the solitary glands, in
the villi, some of those upon the surface of mucous membranes, some in connection with muscle, nerve, bone, cartilage, and some other tissues, are of this nature, and consist
of living germinal matter, with mere traces of soft formed
material around each mass.   There is no structure through
which these soft living particles, or small portions of living
matter detached from them, may not make their way.   The
destruction of tissue may be very quickly effected by the
growth and multiplication of such masses of germinal
matter.   Many of the changes in disease result from the
undue growth of this substance, and indeed there is no
operation peculiar to living beings in which germinal or
living matter does not take part.   Any sketch of the structure of the cell would be incomplete without an account of
some of the essential alterations which occur in it in disease.
I propose, therefore, to refer very briefly to the general
nature of some of the most important morbid changes.

Within certain limits, the conditions under which cells
ordinarily live may be modified without any departure from
the healthy state, but if the conditions be very considerably
changed, *disease* may result, or the cell may die.   For
instance, if cells, which in their normal state grow slowly,
be supplied with an excess of nutrient pabulum, and increase
in number very quickly, a *morbid* state is engendered.   Or
if, on the other hand, the rate at which multiplication takes

place be reduced in consequence of an insufficient supply of nourishment, or from other causes, a diseased state may result. So that, in the great majority of cases, *disease* or the *morbid state* essentially differs from health or the healthy state in an increased or reduced rate of growth and multiplication of the germinal matter of one or more particular tissues or organs. In the process of *inflammation*, in the formation of *inflammatory products*, as *lymph and pus*, in the production of *tubercle* and *cancer*, we see the results of increased multiplication of the germinal matter of the tissues or of the germinal matter derived from the blood, consequent upon the appropriation of *excess of nutrient pabulum*. In the shrinking, and hardening, and wasting which occur in many tissues and organs in disease, we see the effects of the germinal matter of a texture being supplied with too little nutrient pabulum, in consequence sometimes of an alteration in the pabulum itself, sometimes of an undue thickening and condensation of the tissue which forms the permeable septum, which intervenes between the pabulum and the germinal matter.

The above observations may be illustrated by reference to what takes place when pus is formed from an epithelial cell, in which the nutrition of the germinal matter, and consequently its rate of growth, is much increased. And the changes which occur in the liver cell in cases of wasting and contraction of that organ (*cirrhosis*) may be advanced as an illustration of a disease which consists essentially in the occurrence of changes at a slower rate than would be the case in the normal condition, consequent upon the normal access of pabulum to the germinal matter being interfered with.

The outer hardened formed material of an epithelial cell may be torn or ruptured mechanically, as in a scratch or prick by insects, pl. VIII, figs. 32 to 35; or it may be rendered soft and more permeable to nutrient pabulum by the action of certain fluids which bathe it. In either case it is clear that *the access of pabulum to the germinal matter must be facilitated,* and the latter necessarily *"grows"*—that is, converts certain of the constituents of the pabulum that come into contact with it into matter like itself—at an increased rate. The mass of germinal matter increases in size, and soon begins to divide into smaller portions, fig. 33. Parts seem to move away from the general mass, fig. 34. These at length become detached, and thus several separate masses of germinal matter, which are embedded in the softened and altered formed material, result, figs. 34, 35. These changes will be understood by reference to the figures in plate VIII. In this way the so-called inflammatory product *pus* results. The abnormal pus-corpuscle is produced from the *germinal or living matter of a normal epithelial cell, the germinal matter of which has been supplied with pabulum much more freely than in the normal state.* In all forms of inflammation, the germinal matter of the parts inflamed increases very much, and the same change occurs in every kind of fever, fig. 36, pl. VIII, but not to the same extent. In both conditions there is increased development of heat due to the increase of the germinal matter. Inflammations and fevers are so very closely related that an inflammation may be spoken of as a *local fever,* and a fever as a *general inflammation.*

It will be seen how easily the nature of the changes occurring in cells in inflammation, fever, and other morbid

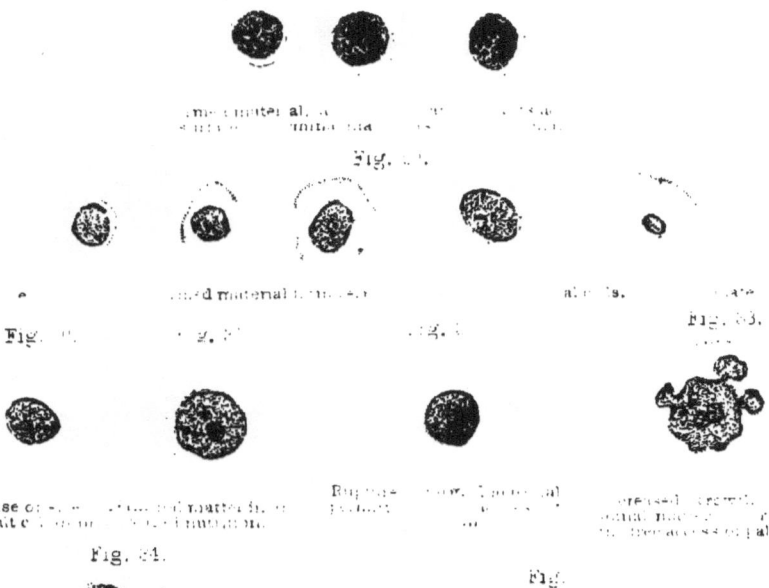

ame material, a . . . .
. . . . mible oid . . . . .

Fig. . .

. . . .d material . . . . . .   a . . 's.   . . . .te

Fig. . .   . . g. .   . . . g. .   Fig. . 3.

rease o . . . . d matter i . . .   Rupt . . . . o . . . al   . . . .
adult c . . . . t i . . . . t . . . .   p . . . .
                                                                                                . . . . o . . al

Fig. . 4.   Fig . . .

ivision and mul . . . . u of a
minal matter ot ad . . . . . l from . .
creased access of pa . . . u . . . . In th . .
way 'pus corpuscles' may be formed
from the germinal matter of . . p . .
thelium

Mul . . . . j . . . . . . uscl . s.

. . g. . 6.

rtio . o . muscle in fever sh . . in . enlargement and mu . . . . of masses of germinal m . .
from . ncreased nutrit . . n   . . . . . . app . . . . . . is comm . . . . fever and inflamma . ion.   x 70 .

F . g. . 7.

. . . . ng and quickly grow . . . . of epithelium . n health or dis . . . . owing
germinal matter and so . . . . . . med material su . . oundi . . . . . .   x . 00.

1000th of an inch .   . x 7 . .

changes, can be explained, if the artificial terms, *cell-wall*, *cell-contents*, *nucleus*, be given up. In all acute internal inflammations and in fevers a much larger quantity of inanimate pabulum is taken up by certain cells and converted into germinal matter than in the normal state. Hence there is, at least in the parts affected, increase in bulk. Cells of particular organs, which live very slowly in health, live very fast in certain forms of disease. More pabulum reaches them, and they grow more rapidly in consequence.

In cells which have been growing very rapidly and are returning to their normal condition, *in which the access of nutrient pabulum is more restricted than in the abnormal state*, as is also the case in normal cells passing from the embryonic to the fully-formed state, the outer part of the germinal matter undergoes conversion into formed material, and this last increases although the supply of pabulum is reduced.

From these observations it follows that disease may result in two ways—either from the cells of an organ growing and multiplying faster than in the normal state, or from their doing so more slowly. In the one case, *the normal restrictions under which growth takes places are diminished; in the other, the restrictions are greatly increased.* *Pneumonia*, or inflammation of the lung, may be adduced as a striking example of the first condition, for in this disease millions of minute masses of germinal matter which have escaped from the blood suspended in liquor sanguinis (exudation) grow and multiply very rapidly in the air cells of the lung, and nutrient constituents are diverted from other parts of the body to this focus of morbid activity. Contraction and condensation of the liver, kidney, and other glands, hardening, shrinking, and wasting of the muscular, nervous, and other tissues, are good examples of the second. The amount of change becomes less and less as the morbid state advances, the whole organ wastes, the secreting structure shrinks, and at last inactive connective tissue alone marks the seat where most active and energetic changes once occurred. It is easy to see how such a substance as alcohol must tend to restrict the rapid multiplication of the cells when the process is too active, and how it would tend to promote the advance of disease in organs where rapid change in the cells characterizes the normal state.

These considerations lead us to conclude that the rate of growth of cells in disease may be accelerated or retarded by an alteration in the character of the pabulum which is transmitted to them, and with the view of influencing these changes we shall naturally search for remedies which have the property of rendering tissues more or less permeable to nutrient fluids, or which alter the character of the fluid itself. Such considerations have a very important bearing upon the practical treatment of disease.

Many of the so-called tonics have the property of coagulating albuminous fluids and solutions of extractive matters. Preparations containing tannin, the mineral salts, such as the sulphate and sesquichloride of iron, nitric and hydrochloric acids, and a host of other remedies that will occur to every one, possess this property, and render solutions containing these and allied substances less permeable, perhaps by increasing their viscidity. The favourable action of such remedies is probably due to their direct influence on the fluid constituents of the blood. They, no doubt, also reduce the rate at which blood-corpuscles are disintegrated, and at the same time they tend to render the walls of the blood-vessels less permeable to fluids.

But, of all remedies, I believe alcohol acts most rapidly in this way, and in these particular cases most efficiently. The properties alcohol possesses of hardening animal tissues, and of coagulating albuminous fluids, are well known; and these properties must not be forgotten when its effects in the animal body are discussed. Of course, when absorbed by the blood, it does not actually coagulate the albuminous matters ; but it probably renders them less fluid, and reduces their permeating property. Alcohol interferes with the disintegration of blood-corpuscles; and in cases where this is going on very rapidly, and where fluid is passing through the walls of the vessels in considerable quantity, in consequence of the walls themselves being stretched and too readily permeable to fluids, alcohol is likely to be of service ; but where these changes are occurring very rapidly, and the patient's strength is fast ebbing, it may save life.

Alkalies, on the other hand, tend to render formed material more permeable to fluids, and thus facilitate the access of pabulum to the germinal matter. They are often useful in cases where there is shrinking and wasting of textures which in the normal condition consist principally of germinal matter. The value of potash, soda, lithia, and their carbonates, as well as the salts of many vegetable acids which become converted into carbonates in the system, act beneficially in this way, as well as producing favourable changes of other kinds.

OF "LIFE."

HAT is to be understood by the term *life:* is a question which has been answered very differently by different authorities in these days, and it is one to which a satisfactory reply has never yet been received. Few words are in more frequent use, and yet it is most difficult to define the meaning of this word *life*, partly no doubt, because it has been used in so many different senses. By the "life" of the world, of a nation, or of a society, we mean something very different from what we mean by the "life" of an individual; for may not many individuals perish without the life of the world, of a nation, or of a society being destroyed or impaired? The "life" of a man, or an animal, is very different from what is termed the "life" of a white blood, or of a mucus, or pus corpuscle; inasmuch as many hundreds of white blood corpuscles, or elemental units of the tissues, might die in the man, without affecting the "life" of the man; moreover the man might die, and some of the corpuscles remain alive.

" Life," as employed in the first instance, comprises a great number of results and changes so complicated, and so different from one another, that volumes might be written without the subject being exhausted. The "life" of a man or an animal includes phenomena of *essentially different kinds*, some being *mechanical* and *chemical*, while others belong to a totally different class. Physical and chemical actions may be investigated in many ways, but so far as we have got, the last class of actions (vital) seems to be beyond investigation, and has not yet been satisfactorily accounted for. If we regard the life of a man, for example, as the sum of all the actions going on in his body, the sum will be made up of a number of very different and heterogeneous items. To sum up these together and express the result in a common total would be as unmeaning as it would be to add ounces to shillings and inches. By the "life" of a white blood corpuscle or other small mass of living matter we mean the property or power or conditions to which the phenomena, characteristic of this and other kinds of matter in the same state, are referable.

Here then are three distinct senses in which the term life has been employed, and more might be adduced. It must, therefore, be obvious that by the *life* of a man some thing very different is understood from what is meant by the life of each elemental unit of his organism, and the difference is not merely of degree but of kind.

We cannot prove that life results from, or is invariably associated with such and such chemical and physical changes, or is due to certain external conditions, and it is easy to adduce instances in which life is present under opposite and conflicting circumstances. In short the conditions under which life exists are so many and so variable that it is not reasonable to attribute it to any conceivable combinations of external circumstances unless we may assume that the very same phenomena result from the concurrence of very different conditions.

F

Is a Tissue living because attached to a Living Organism ?

Some appear to think that a change in position only will make all the difference as regards the proper application of the term *vital*, and seem to hold that a tissue should be called *alive* as long as it remains attached to a living body, *dead* when detached, irrespective of changes occurring in the tissue itself. But it is obvious that a leaf, or an elementary part, may be as devoid of life while it remains attached to the living trunk as after its connection with it has been completely severed. To say that a dead leaf exhibits life as long as it hangs on to the branch would be absurd, because differences of a much more important character proclaim whether the leaf be alive or dead, irrespective of its connection with the tree.

Not long ago, it was stated that a living thing might spring from a dying or dead one, as a fungus from a dead elm, by mere transference of force from the latter to the former,—that the departing life-force of one thing became transformed into the life of the new one.

Chemical and Mechanical Changes in Living Beings.

Neither should changes which are admitted to be *mechanical* and *chemical*, when they occur in the laboratory, be called *vital*, merely because they take place in a living organism. It is the nature of the change alone which determines its vital or non-vital character. But the term *vital* is constantly applied to actions which, for the last fifty years, have been admitted to be mechanical and chemical, and the confusion with regard to the meaning of the word has been further increased by the assertion that mechanical and chemical actions are the *only* actions that are to be called *vital.* Some philosophers have indeed arrived at the conclusion that in truth there are *no vital as distinguished from physical and chemical actions.* Further, it has been held that as we can imitate osmose, oxidize certain substances and produce in the laboratory compounds like those formed in the body, we may prophesy that *all other actions* occurring in living beings *will eventually be imitated.* But it would be as reasonable to maintain that because we can now produce urea we shall by and by be able to form a hair or develop an eye out of the contents of a crucible, or that as we can build up by synthesis very complex organic compounds, ere long we shall be able to make a brain cell which will form ideas. Because we can make many products like those resulting from the disintegration of tissues, does it therefore follow that in the time to come we shall be able to develop an embryo by the admixture of two kinds of albuminous fluids prepared artificially? As oxygen and hydrogen can be made to combine by the contact of platinum, therefore it is said certain combinations of living particles are also examples of catalytic action. Because many actions have been attributed to vitality which are unquestionably physical and chemical, therefore all actions which are now regarded as vital will ultimately be proved to be physical, Those who argue in this way fail to perceive that they are dealing with two different classes or kinds of actions. The truth is physics and chemistry have never advanced one step in the directions indicated. Great things have been done, but in altogether different lines of enquiry. Strange as it may seem many undoubtedly high authorities have for years past failed to distinguish between the act of construction in the case of a machine or an organism, and the work performed by it after its construction is complete. They have failed to recognize any difference between formation and action, and have forgotten that before an organ can act or perform its function, it must be *formed*, and that its function and mode of action are in great measure determined by the changes which occurred during its formation.

The power or force which is concerned in the formation of an organ endowed with the most exquisite faculties is supposed to be of the same essential nature as that which causes certain kinds of matter to assume a definite crystalline form. The formation of organs and structures designed for the fulfilment of definite purposes which must have been foreseen, as it were, from the earliest period of development, is supposed to result from nothing more than the action and reaction of the properties and forces of the elements of matter concerned, and the external conditions to which it is exposed. But it must be borne in mind that temporary structures are first produced which are useless in themselves and only serve as a provisional basis for the development of the masses of germinal matter from which permanent structure is to be evolved.

Actions in Living Beings.

A very little observation will convince us that in the body there are very different kinds of actions proceeding simultaneously. The formation and growth of muscular tissue would seem to be processes essentially distinct from its contraction, and yet both sets of phenomena have been attributed to the influence of the same forces. But building up and breaking down—solution and precipitation—development of structure and its removal—addition of matter to, and removal of matter from, a tissue—have been attributed to the operation of the ordinary forces. But not one of these phenomena as they occur in living beings can be explained by any known laws of physics, or imitated artificially.

" There are no truly vital actions," " there is no life,"—say some, and thus evade further discussion of this momentous question. But it has been shown that there is a marked distinction between the living matter and the formed matter (see p. 32), and that the phenomena going on in these two kinds of matter respectively are essentially different, and can be considered apart from one another. By ignoring altogether this and other important facts of observation, which have been demonstrated of late years, and by calling those who differ from them " vitalists;" by saying that facts opposed to their view are unimportant, and stigmatizing every argument against their doctrines as frivolous, and under cover of jokes about the fiction of vitality, making bold assertions, popular teachers may partially succeed in forcing upon the people the acceptance of dogmas which are utterly untenable. The interest is excited by the very forcible and high-sounding terms employed, but the writing is often remarkable for vagueness and laxity of ex pression, and conspicuous for its complete want of precision and clearness of meaning, and the use of terms that beg the question under consideration.

The matter in dispute has, at least as regards my own observations, been actually misrepresented; for—

1. It has been said that the actions which I have termed *vital* are really physical and chemical.

2. The actions to which I have restricted the term *vital*, and which occur in the germinal matter only, have been completely ignored.

But although the new schools hold it absurd to suppose that any peculiar power acting from within or from without can influence the changes in matter, or direct its forces, they see no impropriety in attributing to matter itself, and to force, guiding and directing, and forming agencies. They transfer to the non-living those active, controlling, and directing powers which have been hitherto considered as limited peculiarly to the living world. It is the inorganic molecule, not *will*, or *mind*, or *power*, which governs, arranges, and guides.

Only recently, Professor Huxley has affirmed that a " particle of jelly" (protoplasm ?) guides forces.* But the Professor has not explained what he means by guiding physical forces. He should have given us some

---

* Mr. Huxley remarks, that to his mind it is a *fact* of the profound-est significance that "this particle of jelly (!) is capable of guiding physical forces in such a manner as to give rise to those exquisite and almost mathematically arranged structures," &c.—" Introduction to the Classification of Animals."

idea of the property or force by virtue of which this jelly, this matter, is enabled to guide forces, and how the property was acquired. What are the laws which govern it, and how comes it that physical forces obey matter; what is the nature of the act of guiding spoken of? Does every kind of matter, under certain circumstances, guide forces, or only certain combinations of matter, or only special kinds of matter? Is it due to a mere command that is mysteriously obeyed, or to some repulsion or attraction, or if there be a subtle influence, what is the nature of this, and whence did it come? Here, as in many other cases, Mr. Huxley makes an assertion which he expects his pupils to receive without telling them the grounds he has for making it. No doubt Mr. Huxley feels quite satisfied that what he states is true. He speaks so authoritatively about *fact* and *law* ("fact I know, and law I know,") that one scarcely dares to venture to beg for an explanation of anything Mr. Huxley has affirmed.

But many students ask if Mr. Huxley's "facts" have been confirmed, and are anxious to learn something concerning the evidence upon which they are supposed to rest. *Why* should the idea of jelly guiding forces be a *fact* of profound significance, and the idea of "vitality" acting upon the particles of this jelly, and guiding them and their forces, be a *fiction*, frivolous, absurd, ridiculous, fanciful, &c.? Again; some think that physical forces guide matter, but here we have the new doctrine taught that matter guides physical forces. But it may be that neither matter nor force is capable of guiding or directing force or matter.

Mr. Huxley agrees with those who attribute to matter itself that which has been attributed by others to power acting upon the matter. One view is, that matter guides and rules itself of itself; another, that matter is guided and ruled by something acting upon it.

Concerning the dictum about jelly guiding physical forces, I shall venture to remark—1. That living matter is not jelly; 2. That neither jelly nor *matter* is capable of *guiding* or *directing* forces of any kind; and 3. That the capacity of jelly to guide forces, which Professor Huxley says is a *fact* of the profoundest significance to him, is not a *fact* at all, but merely an assertion.

Living matter is first called a name given to non-living matter; then it is asserted that this does so and so, which it has never been proved to do; this is next stated to be a fact of the profoundest significance; and by such devices the public is taught to believe in the creative and directing power of the non-living. Arguments of another kind have already led many to accept as an article of faith the dogma, that it is force alone which forms and builds, and designs and makes; and that the only source of the countless living things which people this earth is the sun,—" the God of this new world."

ACTIONS CHARACTERIZING EVERY KIND OF LIVING MATTER, BUT NEVER OCCURRING IN ANY FORM OF NON-LIVING MATTER.

Let us now proceed to inquire whether there are any characters or phenomena which are common to all kinds of matter that lives, and manifested by this only. All living matter *grows*, and *moves*, and *forms*, of its own accord, while non-living matter cannot be made to do any of these things. Hence it is fair to say that growth, spontaneous movement, and formation are *vital phenomena*. We cannot at present conceive of life without a capacity for these phenomena. The actions may remain dormant for a time, but when circumstances are favourable, they manifest themselves very distinctly. Although in many cases *these vital phenomena* may be hidden and obscured by very evident physical and chemical changes, we shall invariably find evidence of them. By tracing the various actions in living beings towards their source, we shall always find that these vital actions underlie the rest, and contribute in a most important measure to the results we are able to observe, study, and investigate. And as neither growth, spontaneous movement, nor formation, have been imitated artificially, or known to occur in non-living matter, or proved to result from physical actions, I attribute these phenomena to *vitality*, or *vital power or force*, or to *life*, until a more satisfactory explanation shall be discovered.

I regard this *" vitality "* as a power of a peculiar kind,

exhibiting no analogy whatever to any known forces. It cannot be a *property* of matter, because it is in all respects essentially different in its actions from all acknowledged properties of matter. The vital property belongs to a different category altogether.

That the properties of elements which disappear, or are changed when compounds are formed, are really retained, can be proved, because when each element is again isolated it manifests its elemental properties ; but the *vital properties* are lost whenever living matter dies, and are never regained by the same particles. The vital actions of the highest and lowest known forms of living matter appear to be of the same essential nature, although the results of vital actions upon the form, properties, and composition of the material produced are very different in different organisms. But between the vital actions of the simplest and most degraded forms of living matter, and any actions that are known to occur under the most complex circumstances, in non-living matter, there appears to be no analogy whatever. Instead of attributing the phenomena peculiar to living beings to any force or power of a peculiar or special kind, it is considered more in accordance with the " tendencies " of scientific investigation in these days, and much more philosophical to assert that the phenomena which I have called *vital* are the consequences of antecedent physical phenomena.

When one portion of a mass of living matter is seen to move in advance of other portions it may be said that the movement is due to some phenomenal alteration which occurred just before. But what evidence have we that this change which cannot be rendered evident to our senses was really *phenomenal?* This movement is one of the essential attributes of living matter. We cannot conceive of living matter without the capacity for such movement. The growth of the forest could no more be accomplished without this wonderful power of movement which overcomes the attraction of gravitation, than the changes in form of the simplest living particles, or the active movement of the vibrio or the vibration of a cilium. The visible changes which occur in the form of a mass of germinal or living matter undoubtedly succeed and are a consequence of *antecedent* changes, but what do we know about these antecedent changes? All we have learnt positively is that the matter moves in a manner peculiar to matter of this kind. Shall we account for the movement by saying—that it is a consequence of antecedent phenomena—or that it is due to an inherent tendency to move—or to a property which it has derived from matter like it from which it came—or to some mysterious agency acting from without or from within, or to the action and reaction of forces acting in both directions? It is not possible to *prove* why the matter moves because we have no means of investigating its state just prior to the occurrence of the actual movement, but the universality of this movement in the living world convinces us that it is of the highest importance and very intimately related to life itself. This movement has been shown to be peculiar and so far has not been excited in any form of non-living matter. Is it not, therefore, reasonable to suppose that the condition which immediately precedes the occurrence of actual movement is also peculiar to living matter? But is it a *phenomenal*

change ? Some action, state, or condition, must undoubtedly take place in the matter just prior to movement,
differing from the condition or state which obtains in the
living matter when no movement is about to occur, but we
cannot demonstrate any difference whatever; neither have
we yet been able to discover any means by which the state
of change just preceding active movement can be distinguished from the state of ordinary and comparative rest.
We do not in fact know when a movement is about to
occur, we only know the fact of its occurrence. If the
state just preceding movement is to be attributed to antecedent phenomena, the state of rest might with equal propriety be attributed to the very same antecedent phenomena.
It is doubtful if the word phenomenon is at all applicable
to the supposed change in the relations of the particles of
living matter which results in actual movement. Is it
correct to speak of a condition or state which cannot be
rendered evident to the senses, as a phenomenon ? A
certain change common to every kind of living matter
occurs just prior to the movement of its particles which
universally distinguishes this from every other known state
of matter. As the movement is peculiar, its cause must be
peculiar, and it seems more reasonable to attribute this to
some peculiar power manifested by living matter only, than
to an antecedent phenomenon which is different in its
essential nature from every other action or change to which
the term phenomenon has been applied. In truth, when
we enter upon the consideration of the cause of the
changes in living matter, we soon get beyond the limits of
observation and experiment. It may of course be said that

such discussions are therefore futile and out of the province of science. But if this view be accepted we must cease to enquire almost as soon as we have commenced to investigate. In that case the consideration of the growth, formation and action of the simplest being, and of every elementary unit entering into the formation of the tissues of every living creature must be as a sealed book. And it would be absurd to attempt to describe the processes of growth, formation and secretion, as they occur in living beings. The question not only lies at the very root of physiology, but forces itself upon our consideration at every step. It must, therefore, be discussed, and provisional hypotheses may be advanced if only to mark the paths already traversed in the course of our difficult and never-ending exploration.

That the physical school should try to stop all enquiry at this very point is exactly what might be expected, for the subject is obviously out of the path of physical enquiry, but it by no means, therefore, follows that nothing is to be learnt concerning it. No wonder that those who would have us believe that the highest aspirations of the soul are but manifestations of so many units of force, desire to chain the mind so tightly to the material that it shall no longer exercise one of its remarkable endowments— that of stretching towards regions into which the senses cannot penetrate. Is the mind to follow the senses, instead of leading, controlling, and directing them? Are the senses to govern the intellect and to dictate to it the conditions under which it may work? But even the disciples of the physical school cannot altogether refrain from advancing vain speculations and fanciful hypotheses. Is it then the attempt to speculate in one particular direction that gives such offence in these days, and which ought to be put down, with the utmost firmness? The new school professes to consider all enquiries worthless which are not conducted by experiment and observation, and yet how many obscure and doubtful facts of observation and experiment are advanced and used as scientific certainties, when the magic light of physical theory has been projected upon them? It is indeed very desirable to bring us face to face with "facts," but it is astonishing how many grand facts of the profoundest significance are slowly resolved into harmless fictions of the imagination condensed and duly concentrated into very strong language to suit the dictates of a party determined to make people think in one way only, or to prevent them from thinking at all. But the authoritative language of opponents need not deter us from entering upon the discussion of a matter which is of more than ordinary interest to all, and I shall venture to draw certain conclusions concerning the probable nature of life; although I can only receive indirect assistance from observation and experiment.

OF VITALITY.

How are we to explain the wonderful changes which take place in the germinal or living matter, and how are we to account for the capacity which this exhibits of passing through orderly series of changes, the last of which seems to have been provided for, and, as it were, anticipated from the very first?

There is in living matter nothing which can be called a mechanism, nothing in which structure can be discerned. A little transparent colourless material is the seat of these marvellous powers or properties by which the form, structure, and function of the tissues and organs of all living things are determined. But this transparent material possesses a remarkable power of movement as has been already referred to. See page 39. It may thus transport itself long distances, and extend itself so as to get through pores, holes, and canals too minute to be seen even with the aid of very high powers. There are creatures of exquisite tenuity which are capable of climbing through fluids and probably through the air itself—creatures which climb without muscles, nerves or limbs—creatures with no mechanism, having no structure, capable when suspended in the medium in which they live, of extending any one part of the pulpy matter of which they consist beyond another part, and of causing the rest to follow. As if each part *willed* to move and did so, or moved in immediate response to mandates operating upon it from a distance, governed by some undiscovered, and at present unimagined laws,—creatures which multiply by separating into two or more parts without loss of substance, or capacity, or power. It would seem that each part possessed equal powers with the whole, for the smallest particle detached may soon grow into a body like the original mass in every respect; and the process may be repeated infinitely without any loss or diminution in capacity or power. It may be asked if there is anything approaching this occurring within the range of physics or chemistry.

Of a Living Spherule.

Let us imagine we could look into the ultimate particles of the living, active, moving matter, and consider what we should probably discern. I think we should see spherules of extreme minuteness, each composed of still smaller spherules, and these of spherules infinitely minute. Such spherules have upon their surface a small quantity of matter differing in properties from that in the interior, but so soft and diffluent that the particles may come into very close proximity. In each little spherule the matter is in active movement, and new minute spherules are being formed in its central part, and these are making their way outwards so as to give place for the formation of new ones, which are continually appearing in the centre of every one of the living particles. The rate of growth of the entire mass varies with the rate at which the new particles are evolved in the centre.

Each spherical particle is free to move in fluid, and the intervals between the particles are occupied by fluid. This fluid contains, in solution,—

1. Matter about to become living;

2. Substances which exert a chemical action, but do not necessarily form a constituent part of the living mass, together with particles which are rejected, and not capable of being animated; and

3. Substances resulting from the changes ensuing in particles which have arrived at the end of their period of existence, and the compounds formed by the action of oxygen upon these.

There can be no doubt that the smallest particle of living matter is complex. It is impossible to conceive the existence of a living particle of any simple substance like iron, oxygen, nitrogen, &c.; for *living* involves changes in which several different elements take part. It seems to me, therefore, that the term *living atom* cannot with propriety be employed, seeing that *living matter* is of complex composition, while the idea of an *atom* seems to involve simplicity of constitution, if not indivisibility. The whole question of the arrangement and form of the atoms in living matter can at present only be discussed theoretically; and I would now merely remark with reference to this subject, that although all living particles are of complex composition, many different elements may exist in very different proportions in living matter; and that there is reason to believe that the smallest particles of *every kind* of living matter are spherical. It is not possible to see, with the highest powers now made, particles which would in all probability be demonstrable by more perfect glasses. But there is reason to think that in any case we must fail to see the actual particles, which are the seat of change, in consequence of their extreme tenuity and transparency. The further consideration of this question is of the deepest interest; but from this point the inquiry assumes a too purely speculative character for me to pursue it here, as I am anxious not to diverge very far from the consideration of phenomena which can be investigated by observation and experiment. It seems however to me probable that the wonderful changes occurring when inanimate matter becomes living, which occur in living beings alone,

G

take place in the central part of the spherical particles of germinal matter only. Discussions as to the nature of the vital forces must, I think, therefore be confined to the consideration of the changes which take place in those minute living spherules of which there is reason to believe we can only see some which are comparatively of large size, and probably many series removed from their ultimate spherical components.

Centrifugal Movement of Living Particles.

Movement takes place in the most minute living particles in a direction from centre to circumference, while the inanimate matter which is about to become living passes in the opposite direction ; or, in other words, the inanimate matter passes into the centre of a particle which already lives, becomes *living*, and then moves outwards. The flow of the inanimate matter is *centripetal*, and the movement of the living matter is *centrifugal.* But both sets of movements are to be accounted for by the centrifugal tendency of the living matter ; for it is obvious that as it thus tends to move from a centre, a flow in the opposite direction must be induced. Such tendency to move from a centre, it would seem, must be due to a force very different from that which controls the movements of inanimate matter. Moreover, while cosmical force influences masses of the largest magnitude and of infinite minuteness, through varying distance, the vital forces can only exert their sway when the distance is infinitely slight ; and it would seem that this influence can only affect matter which is brought into the very centre of the living particle.

Alteration in Vital Power.

It is remarkable that the results of the act of living in different masses of germinal matter having the same origin should be very different. And in the development of new centres one within the other, the masses last produced seem to have acquired powers which their progenitors did not possess. In the formation of the ovum itself the production of centre within centre proceeds for a long time before the actual mass from which the new being is to be evolved is produced. On the other hand, thousands of masses of germinal matter are formed during the early periods of development, which apparently only serve the purpose of giving origin within themselves to others from which those which are to take part in the formation of tissues are at length developed. Thus, many successive series of masses of germinal matter are formed, and are succeeded by new ones before those by which the tissue or organ is to be formed are produced. And these result from the development of new centres or nuclei within already existing living matter. Each successive series of nuclei seems to acquire new power, although there are no characters by which it could be distinguished from any pre-existing or succeeding series. That there is a difference is, however, proved by the difference in the results of living. Moreover, at the same time that the new centre acquires new powers, it retains by inheritance some of those possessed by the germinal matter that preceded it, and hands these down to the new centres it originates. It would, therefore, appear more in accordance with the facts to conclude that the

G 2

powers exhibited by the last of a series of masses of germinal matter were somehow retained in relation with· the matter of every one of its predecessors, and thus handed down from generation to generation, than to assume that the new powers were acquired in consequence of the different series being successively exposed to different external conditions. But this last view is really untenable, because we have abundant evidence of the transmission of peculiar properties and powers, through a vast number of successive units during a considerable period of time, and though sometimes dormant for a while, they are yet at last manifested so distinctly that no doubt could be entertained as to their actual transmission from particle to particle.

New Centres not formed by Aggregation.

It cannot be supposed that the new centres of living matter are in any way formed by the aggregation of particles derived from distant parts ; for, if this were so, these living particles must have traversed formed material, and passed to the very centre of the living germinal matter. But we have ample evidence to prove that the movement of living particles is in one direction only, *from* and not *towards* centres. Moreover, there is reason to think that the only matter passing towards centres is *dissolved non-living pabulum*, and if living particles were suspended in this, they would be filtered off by the formed material, and would never reach the living matter. The arrangement is such as to permit fluid only to go to the living matter, and check the passage of all insoluble particles of whatever kind. While, if we admitted as possible the aggregation of millions of particles having different properties and powers, we should still be quite unable to explain how it is that they did not interfere with one another's interests; why, for instance, the most vigorous did not grow at the expense of their weaker brethren, starving them by appropriating their pabulum, destroying them utterly, and occupying the space which they had not the strength to retain.

Increased Action.

Increase in formative and constructive power seems to be associated with the most limited change in germinal matter, while rapid change—increased vital action—seems to be invariably connected with decadence in power. How can such phenomena be in any way due to the influence of the ordinary forces associated with lifeless matter? No form or mode of force yet discovered has been known to act in any way at all analogous to this. The results must, therefore, be attributed to some peculiar power capable of controlling and directing both matter and force.

It has been suggested that the different substances and different structures produced by germinal matter at different periods of development may depend upon the different surrounding conditions present when the changes occur. This, however, is no explanation at all, for the surrounding conditions to which a mass of living matter in a growing organism is exposed, as well as the circumstances concerned in the production of these, are complex. They are not simple external conditions, but are in part the result of external circumstances, and in part of a previous state of things in the establishment of which pre-existing vital powers, associated with germinal matter, played no unimportant part. It has been shown that the production of formed matter is due to the death of living matter under certain conditions, which is itself a highly complex phenomenon, and cannot be explained without supposing—

1. Certain *internal* forces capable of causing the elements of the matter to arrange themselves in a certain definite manner totally different from that in which the ordinary forces of matter would cause these elements to be arranged; and

2. Certain *influences operating from without* (*i.e.*, surrounding external conditions) tending to prevent the supposed internal forces from exerting their sway. The composition, structure and properties of the matter produced, must, it seems to me, be referred to the influence of very different antagonistic forces acting upon matter in opposite directions. All this, which takes place in all living particles, seems very different from anything going on in non-living matter.

Hypothesis of Vital Force.

It seems to me that the facts cannot be accounted for except on the hypothesis of the existence of some force or power which influences, in a manner we do not yet understand, the ultimate elements of matter, and causes them to take up particular relations to one another so that when they combine, compounds of a special kind, and possessing special characters, shall be formed. For, surely it cannot be maintained that the atoms arrange themselves, and devise what positions each is to take up,—and it would be yet more extravagant to attribute to ordinary force or energy, atomic rule and directive agency. We might as well try to make ourselves believe that the laboratory fire made and lighted itself, that the chemical compounds put themselves into the crucible, and the solutions betook themselves to the beakers in the proper order, and in the exact proportions required to form certain definite compounds. But while all will agree that it is absurd to ignore the chemist in the laboratory, many insist upon ignoring the presence of anything representing the chemist in the living matter which they call the "cell-laboratory." In the one case the chemist works and guides, but in the other, it is maintained, the lifeless molecules of matter are themselves the active agents in developing vital phenomena.

Some have taught that mind transcends life, and life transcends chemistry, just as chemical affinity transcends mechanics. But no one has proved, and no one can prove, that mind and life are in any way related to chemistry and mechanics. If the step from mechanics to chemistry is known, has been proved, and is admitted, that from chemistry to life is assumed, and assumed without the slightest reason. If it had been shown that there was some sort of relation between A and B, and another sort of relation between C D, would any one venture to argue that, therefore, B and C must be related ? Neither can it be said that life works *with* physical and chemical forces, for there is no evidence that this is so. On the other hand it is quite certain that life overcomes, in some very remarkable and unknown manner, the influence of physical forces and chemical affinities. Does the tree grow away from the earth or its roots into it, in obedience to the laws of gravitation? Are certain things taken up from the soil and others rejected, or do the leaf cells tear away from carbonic acid its carbon, and drive off its oxygen by reason of chemical affinity? Of course, it will be said that capillary attraction, osmose and other forces, contribute in a highly complex manner to bring about the results; but every one at all acquainted with the subject knows, that the facts have not been, and cannot be explained. Such questions are usually evaded by those who profess to explain them. I ask for one single instance in which the phenomena actually occurring in any living thing, or in a particle of living matter, can be adequately explained by physics and chemistry. The only answer I get is, that if the pheno· mena cannot be explained now, it is certain they will be at no very distant period. One must, however, acquire prodigious physical faith before one can hope to believe that prophetic physics and chemistry are as worthy of acceptance and as convincing to the reason as facts of observation and experiment.

If the explanation of the facts by calling in the aid of some agency, force, or power totally distinct from ordinary force is unsatisfactory, is it not more unsatisfactory, nay, is it not even false, to attribute them to the action of the ordinary cosmical forces, concerning which much is known, but which have never been proved to be capable of effecting any changes at all like those which occur in every kind of living matter?

And it would surely be more in accordance with the true spirit of science, at least while our knowledge remains very imperfect, to study still more carefully the phenomena of the simplest known forms of living matter than to affirm boastingly, that not only these phenomena but those manifested by the highest form living matter is known to take, undoubtedly, result from the influence of mere force which never made a brick or formed a wheel, but yet is held capable of constructing those most wonderful and most beautiful mechanisms which could never have been conceived by the most vivid imagination, but which are being revealed to us in new multitudes day by day in glorious perfection. Surely, these no more result from the fortuitous or force-impelled aggregation of atoms than pictures, statues, mills, or ships do.

If, then, we take a general survey of the phenomena peculiar to living things, I think we shall find ourselves compelled by the facts to accept some such inferences as the following :—

In all living beings there exists matter in a peculiar state which we call *living*. This living matter manifests phenomena which are different from any phenomena proved to be due to the operation of any known laws. It moves in a manner which cannot be explained by physics. Changes are effected in its composition which cannot be accounted for, and various substances are formed by it which may exhibit structure, properties, and a capacity for acting in a manner which is peculiar to living beings, and cannot be imitated artificially or satisfactorily explained. It takes up non-living matter in solution, and communicates its wonderful properties to it. Having increased to a certain size, the mass of living matter divides into smaller portions, every one of which possesses the same properties as the the parent mass, and in equal degree.

Scientific investigators have hitherto failed to discover any laws by which these facts may be accounted for. But rather than ignore or misrepresent them, or affirm anything concerning them which we cannot prove, as some have done, it seems to me preferable to resort provisionally to hypothesis. In order to account for the facts, I conceive that some directing agency of a kind peculiar to the living world exists in association with every particle of living matter, which, in some hitherto unexplained manner, affects temporarily its elements, and determines the precise changes which are to take place when the living matter again comes under the influence of certain external conditions.

In higher animals, besides giving rise to the phenomena above referred to every instant during life in every part of the organism, this supposed agency or power, acting under certain circumstances at an early period of development, so disposes the material which it governs, that mechanisms result of most wonderful structure, admirably adapted, as they have been evidently actually designed, for the fulfilment of definite purposes. These mechanisms were anticipated, as it were, from the earliest period, and their formation provided for by the preparatory changes through which the structures had to pass before perfect development could be attained. Can these phenomena be accounted for except through the influence of some wonderful power or agency such as we are now contemplating?

Of all organic mechanism, the most perfect, the most exalted, and as regards mere structure the most elaborate, is the nervous. Widely diffused, intimately concerned in the actions going on in various tissues, and co-extensive with most of these, it sends filaments to the very confines of the organism. Through this mechanism alone, the very last to be perfected, external changes affect the peculiar form of living matter with which it is in the closest relation, and are thus rendered evident to the living being. The changes occurring in the central living matter of the nervous apparatus may give rise to secondary, combined, and complex actions, through which various ends may be accomplished. These internal impulses are themselves the movements of the particles of the living matter induced by the supposed vital power or agency acting upon them.

In animals yet higher in the scale of creation, the nervous mechanism through which alone the vital power influences other tissues, so as to give rise to associated and combined acts, is still more perfect and elaborate ; but it is formed according to and acts upon the same principles. Actions most complex are carried out through the influence of what is ordinarily termed *will*. This is essentially related to life itself, and probably is the *vital force or power* of certain kinds of living matter. But it must not be supposed that vital phenomena are due to will alone, for in all cases these occur long before there are any manifestations of will, as the term is ordinarily understood,—indeed, before the tissues through which alone *will* operates have been developed. At all periods of life there are tissues which live and grow independent of the influence of *will*. Neither can *instinct* nor *mind* be regarded as *life*, although I think these, as well as *will*, are forms of *vital power*.

In man there seems to be seated in and limited to

a special part of his nervous mechanism, a still higher and more wonderful power, influencing a very special and easily destructible living matter. By virtue of this power man alone, of all created beings, is impelled to seek for the causes of the phenomena he observes, and is enabled to devise new arrangements of material substances for his own definite purposes, and in a manner in which these substances were never arranged before, and in which it is not conceivable they could be arranged without man's design and agency. The power supposed,totally distinct from any forces or properties of which we are cognizant, and not in any way correlated with any known forms or modes of force of which we have any experience,—exerts its sway upon any definite portion of matter, during varying but usually only very brief periods of time, often momentarily, and is then transferred to, or passes on, and influences new particles. From these the powers are transmitted to others, and so on. The amount of matter influenced at any one moment being greater in some situations than in others, and varying according to a number of circumstances. In relation with the delicate living matter, seated near the surface of the grey matter of the convolutions of man's brain, which is alone concerned in mental action, I conceive that vital power attains its most exalted form. It seems to be temporarily chained, as it were, to this matter, which it acts upon, and through which alone it can make itself evident; but seeing that all forms of vital power are transferable, surely there is nothing contrary to reason in supposing that at least this, the highest form, may be freed from the material, and yet exist without cessation, extinction, or annihilation.

LONDON: HARRISON AND SONS,
PRINTERS IN ORDINARY TO HER MAJESTY,
ST. MARTIN'S LANE.

NEW WORKS BY THE SAME AUTHOR.

THE PHYSIOLOGICAL ANATOMY & PHYSIOLOGY OF MAN.

By ROBERT B. TODD, WILLIAM BOWMAN, & LIONEL S. BEALE,

Fellows of the Royal Society.

Being a New Edition, by Dr. BEALE, of Vol. I. of the original Work of Messrs. TODD and BOWMAN. Part I., with Plates, now ready, 7s. 6d. Part II., *nearly ready.*

LONGMANS AND CO.

Cloth, 8vo., 16s.

CLINICAL LECTURES,

By the late ROBERT B. TODD, M.D., F.R.S., formerly Physician to King's College Hospital, and Professor of Physiology and of General and Morbid Anatomy in King's College, London.

Second Edition. Edited by Dr. BEALE.

Now ready, fourth thousand, 16s.

THE USE OF THE MICROSCOPE IN MEDICINE.

FOR PRACTITIONERS AND STUDENTS.

3rd Edition.

This work contains 58 Plates, containing many new Figures, now published for the first time.

Now ready, 25s.

KIDNEY DISEASES, URINARY DEPOSITS, AND CALCULOUS DISORDERS;

AND ON THE TREATMENT OF URINARY DISEASES.

3rd Edition.

Uniform with "The Microscope in its application to Practical Medicine."

THE ARCHIVES OF MEDICINE.

A Record of Practical Observations and Anatomical and Chemical Researches connected with the Observation and Treatment of Disease. Edited by Dr. BEALE.

Vols. I., II., III., and IV. Vols. I. and II., 15s. each; III., 11s.; and IV., 13s. Subscription for four numbers, constituting a volume, 10s.

All Communications and Subscriptions to be addressed to the Editor, King's College, London.

JOHN CHURCHILL AND SONS.

Recently Published,

I.—ON THE STRUCTURE AND FORMATION OF CERTAIN NERVOUS CENTRES,

Tending to prove that the Cells and Fibres of every Nervous Apparatus form an uninterrupted Circuit.

Quarto, 8 Plates, containing 46 Figures, 5s.

II.—INDICATIONS OF THE PATHS TAKEN BY THE NERVE CURRENTS

As they traverse the Caudate Nerve Cells of the Cord and Encephalon.
One Plate and 4 Figures, 1s. 6d.

NEW WORKS PREPARING,

ON THE GERMINAL OR LIVING MATTER OF THE TISSUES AND FLUIDS OF LIVING BEINGS,

An introduction to the Study of Physiology and Medicine.
Being the First Course of Lectures delivered at Oxford by direction of the Radcliffe Trustees.

DISEASE; ITS NATURE & TREATMENT,

INCLUDING

NEW RESEARCHES ON INFLAMMATION AND FEVER, AND ON THE NATURE OF CONTAGIUM,

With Observations on the Cattle Plague and on Cholera. Numerous Plates.

Preparing for Publication, uniform with " Kidney Diseases, Urinary Deposits, and Calculous Disorders," and the " Microscope in Medicine."

THE DISEASES OF THE LIVER AND THEIR TREATMENT.

Including the Anatomy of the Organ in Man and Vertebrate Animals. With upwards of 50 Plates of original Drawings, being a second edition of the Author's Work on the Liver.

JOHN CHURCHILL AND SONS.

All these Works contain the results of the Author's original investigations. They are illustrated with upwards of 2,000 new Engravings, all carefully copied from the actual objects, and most of which have been drawn on wood by the Author himself.

HARRISON AND SONS, PRINTERS IN ORDINARY TO HER MAJESTY, ST. MARTIN'S LANE.